GRACIE'S
SONG

To Nana –
Happy Reading!
Michelle Schlicher

Michelle Schlicher

Published by Michelle Schlicher
ISBN: 978-0-9965750-4-1

Copyright © Michelle Schlicher, 2016

Ebook formatting by Guido Henkel

Printed in the U.S.A.

For Justin,
I'd sing a million songs for you if I could sing.

1.

"YOU'RE IN ROOM 381."

Gracie Brannen smiled politely as she reached out for the key. "Thank you."

Brushing her hair behind her ear, she let her fingers run through the ends, which barely touched her shoulders. Her thick bangs were matted down by the baseball cap she had been wearing before she stepped into the hotel. She fluffed them, letting the air hit her forehead. It was hot for July. While summers in the south could be brutal, this one, especially unkind, seemed unrelenting.

The front desk clerk rambled on, but Gracie's thoughts were elsewhere. She was back. After all these years she was finally back in Glenwood. She looked around the hotel lobby. It was clean, but that was about the only thing it had going for it. The colors were outdated. The lighting awful. But it was the cheapest place in town, and for now, it would do.

The clerk looked up from his computer for a moment, finally pausing after explaining every possible thing to do within a few miles from here. Gracie could have done the spiel herself, considering not much had changed in ten years.

"So, are you in town for business or pleasure?" he asked. Gracie eyed his nametag. Huck. How very Glenwood.

"Business," Gracie replied. "Family business."

"Ah," Huck said, giving her a look like he knew what that meant. He didn't.

"So, where am I?" she asked, changing the subject.

He leaned over the counter and pointed over her shoulder. "Just head down that hallway there. On the left, you'll see stairs. On the right's an elevator. Go up to the third floor and go down the hallway to your right."

She gave him a half-smile and turned to go. She'd almost made it out of sight when she heard him call out to her.

"Let us know if we can help with anything—anything at all."

She glanced back and nodded. "Of course. Thank you."

"Oh, and welcome to Glenwood."

She didn't correct him.

As she headed up the stairs to her room, her legs began to ache from the long car ride. Somehow she'd managed to drive through the night, but she could feel herself hitting a wall. Not only did her legs feel like jelly, but her eyelids were drooping to the point that she thought she might not be able to read the room numbers on the doors she passed.

Arriving at room 381, she pushed the key card in and waited for the green blinking light. Nothing. She tried again, and this time she felt the heavy door push back against her as she leaned in to open it. She didn't look around the room to check out what would be her new home for the next few days. She dropped her bag on the ground, placed her purse on the table in the corner, slipped off her shoes and sank onto the bed. It in no way resembled the plush beds found in more upscale venues. But, to Gracie, at the moment, it felt like heaven.

As she drifted off, her thoughts went back to the desk clerk's last words to her. *Welcome to Glenwood.*

Yes, Gracie, she thought as she drifted off to sleep.

Welcome home.

When Gracie opened her eyes a few hours later, her head hurt. She felt like she'd been sleeping for days. Sitting up on the bed, she stretched her arms out long, yawning at the same time. She glanced over at the clock. 2 p.m. Still enough time to get something done today. It would be two days until the funeral, which was being held on Monday afternoon, and she had some things to attend to before then.

Standing, Gracie spotted her purse on the counter near the entrance to her room, where she'd discarded it on her way to the bed. Her phone stuck out of the top where the zipper wouldn't close, because Gracie always underestimated the amount of stuff she needed to lug around. She put her hands on her hips, thinking. Who should she call first? Or, maybe more importantly, who did she want to see? She knew who she should call, but right now she didn't want to face her. Hannah. Beautiful Hannah. She had stayed in Glenwood to care for their now-deceased mother. Gracie knew it was wrong, but the impending conversation—which was sure to be full of anger and resentment—made her stomach churn.

She walked over to the table and pulled out the slim smartphone. Olivia might be the safest call right now. She had been, after all, one of Gracie's closest confidantes once upon a time.

The phone rang twice before she heard Olivia's sweet voice on the other end.

"Hello?"

Gracie took a deep breath. "Yeah. I'm here," she stammered. "Hi, Olivia." Her heart was beating fast, but she knew she had to start somewhere. "It's me. Gracie."

There was silence on the other end. Maybe Olivia didn't remember her. Or, maybe this wasn't Olivia after all. Maybe...

"Gracie Brannen!" The words broke Gracie's train of thought, and she felt her cheeks squeeze together as she smiled. "I just knew I'd be hearing from you."

"Yeah, I wasn't sure if this was still your number."

"Oh, honey. I've had the same one forever. I only just got one of those new fancy phones you can surf the Internet with—oh, what was it?—like a month ago."

Gracie was grinning like a kid on Christmas morning. Olivia sounded just like she remembered.

"I guess you heard about my mom?" Gracie asked.

"I did. I was sorry to hear it. She was a nice lady, from what I remember of her. You see much of her before she passed?"

That overwhelming guilt she'd felt when she first heard the news started creeping in again. "Not really, no."

"Are you back? In Glenwood, I mean?"

"Yeah. Drove all night if you can believe it. Haven't done that since that camping our senior year."

"Oh gosh, I haven't thought about that in ages! The year I found out I was not a fan of sleeping outdoors!"

Gracie let out a giggle, glad to have the conversation shift away from her mother.

"That was some fun, though," Olivia said. "So, where are you staying?"

"I'm at the Kirkwood."

"Alright. Well, I've got to pick the kids up from camp in about an hour and a half. Grant can watch them after that. He'll be back by four. Can you meet up around then?"

"I haven't got any plans, so yes. I would love to."

"Great," Olivia said.

"So, you and Grant—you two..."

"Yeah, we're still together. Had our ups and downs over the years, but he never could get rid of me." Olivia let out a laugh, robust and full. It made Gracie's heart hurt in a way that it hadn't in a long time.

"That's not surprising," Gracie said. "You two were always crazy about each other."

"Almost as crazy in love as you and Finn. You know, out of everyone, we all thought it'd be you two to end up together."

Gracie flinched at the sound of Finn's name. He was just one of the many loose ends that Gracie left here in Glenwood.

"How is Finn? Settled down now?" She tried to sound nonchalant.

"Not at all. He's working over in Ashland. He's a big-city guy now. Making the big bucks. We still get him down here every once in a while, though. We can't let him forget where he came from, ya know what I mean?"

So, Finn Miller was a booming success in the big city? While it wasn't completely surprising, it wasn't what Gracie had expected either. She shook her head at the silly thought. What had she expected? After all these years that he would still be pining away over her?

Gracie fidgeted and changed the subject again. "Where do you want to meet?"

"How about Murphy's Place—that little place off Walker? It's a dive, but it's cheap and not too loud, so we'll be able to catch up. I have so much to ask you."

Murphy's was still open? Things really had stayed the same around here. "I remember it. I'll see you there a little after four then."

"Okay. And Gracie?"

"Yeah?"

"I'm really glad you're back."

"Me too, Olivia." She meant it, she realized as the words flowed out.

Gracie watched the number disappear from the screen as Olivia hung up. She closed her eyes, relieved.

Olivia had been the right call. Her good-natured friend had always been just that. She was undemanding, quick to forgive (which Gracie reminded herself may or may not be the case in this instance—too early to tell), and most of all, she had a pure graciousness that extended to everyone she met. It took a lot for her happy-go-lucky attitude to be anything but.

Gracie set her phone down and moved back toward the bed she'd been sleeping on. She smoothed out the blankets and fluffed up the pillow. When she turned around, she caught a glimpse of herself in the mirror. Her eyes were bloodshot from wearing her contacts while she slept. Her hair was a complete mess. She looked downright awful.

Better get moving, she thought, and quickly disrobed as she made her way to the bathroom. A quick shower and she'd feel good as new. All she needed was a good washing to wipe off the grime of her trip. And then, she'd be off to meet Olivia. It'd be a clean start.

Gracie checked her watch again. While she knew Olivia must be busy, she'd been waiting nearly half an hour. Her eyes darted back to the door as a few new patrons entered and found seats at the bar. She tapped her fingers on the table and adjusted herself in her seat, unable to make herself more comfortable. She cleared her throat and took another drink from her bottle. It was a bit early in the day for drinking, but she wasn't alone in the place. A group of older men had been playing cards at a corner table since she'd arrived, and a young couple, college-aged, Gracie guessed, was sitting at the bar.

Murphy's looked exactly the same now as it had ten years ago. Back then, Gracie and her friends had been underage, but they'd snuck in one cold night in January to celebrate Grant's birthday, ordering a round of drinks and doing their best to seem old enough to be there. The bartender, too busy to scrutinize their newly-acquired ID's, eyed them suspiciously over the course of the night. They'd happily guzzled down their bottles, drinking another round before deciding they'd better count their lucky stars they hadn't been caught, and made their way out of the place. From there, they'd headed to Grant's old farmhouse and spent the rest of the night sitting under the stars. Grant's older brother Eddy, home from college, joined them there, regaling them with stories of campus life. It hit Gracie that night that their lives were all about to change. As they sat listening to Eddy, she realized, with some frustration, she hadn't realized just how much. And when she'd glanced over at Finn to see if he looked at all as worried as she felt, he'd smiled and squeezed her shoulder. Had she smiled back?

At the front of Murphy's, the door swung open and Gracie got a good look at her friend. Olivia had been a rail in school. She'd had the body type of a catwalk model, with long blonde hair. She was still thin, but now she had definition, a few fine lines and a few gray hairs peeking out from behind her golden highlights.

"Olivia," she said, her voice not sounding like her own. She waved, then stepped out of the booth to greet her friend.

"Gracie Brannen! Well, I'll be. I still can't believe it's you. You're a sight for sore eyes, you are." Olivia held out her arms and pulled Gracie into a big bear hug. Then, releasing her, she stepped back to examine her. "Why, you look exactly the same. It's almost like ten years haven't even passed."

"Well, you look the same, too. Maybe a bit more muscular. Been working out?"

"Me? God, no. Don't have the time. It's probably from lifting those sweet peanuts of mine all the time. You'd think they'd outgrow it, but they still like their Mama to carry them around occasionally."

Gracie smiled, sliding back into the booth as Olivia did the same. "I can't believe you're a mother. I mean, I can. I don't know. It's crazy to think about."

"It's crazy, alright. Crazy-town. My house is a zoo, Gracie, and I'm the zookeeper. Grant's as bad as the kids sometimes. He riles 'em up before bed, lets 'em finger paint in the kitchen, then doesn't watch to make sure they don't paint the walls. But he's a good daddy."

"How old are they?" Gracie asked.

"Ezra is seven," she said, sighing, as if it were hard for her to believe it. "Judd is four."

"Wow," she whispered.

Olivia took out her phone, turning it to Gracie so she could see the screen. A picture of two little boys with ruddy cheeks and huge smiles stared back at her. "My pride and joy," Olivia said.

"They're beautiful."

"Thank you. But, like I said, they're a handful." A waitress came by and Olivia ordered a drink. "It's never too early for drinkin' in this town." When the waitress returned with it a few moments later, she took a swig and then met Gracie's eyes. "Now, tell me, Gracie. Where the hell have you been all these years?"

Gracie averted her eyes and felt her cheeks grow warm. She knew she'd have to answer this question, and she'd rehearsed it plenty. But now, sitting across from Olivia, those prepared lines seemed too insincere, too cowardly, and that feeling tripped Gracie up. She stammered, unable to get the right words out.

"Listen, you don't have to tell me if you don't want to. The last thing I want to do is scare you off now that you're finally back."

Gracie glanced up, relieved. "Thank you."

"You'll tell me when you're ready." Olivia winked at her, a friendly truce not to pry for the time being. "So, what can you tell me?"

"Well, I went to nursing school. Just finished a little over a year ago."

"That's really something, Gracie. You're workin' then?"

Gracie nodded. "I am. Doing night shifts at a children's hospital. That's why I drove most of last night. My body's on a bit of a different schedule."

"I bet you're a great nurse. You always were taking care of everybody, now that I think about it. Suits you."

"What about you?"

Olivia smiled, letting her hands fall to her lap. "I'm home right now. I've got my degree, but when I had Ezra, I just couldn't bear to leave him."

Gracie felt her palms grow sweaty. "Well, that's where mamas are supposed to be, aren't they? Caring for their babies?" she asked, coughing to clear out her throat.

"Tell that to my husband."

"Grant doesn't want you home?"

She shrugged. "He misses the extra paycheck, but he's glad they're with me. It'll be another year until Judd goes to kindergarten. He just turned four last month. I guess in another year or so I'll think about finding work again. Part-time if I can."

"What kind of work?"

"Well, if you can believe it, I'm in finance. My last job was at the credit union just down the street, so when I go back it'll probably be to something similar."

When Olivia started laughing, Gracie realized she'd, unintentionally, frowned at her friend's response. "I'm sorry. I didn't mean to…I'm just not a numbers person."

"No need to apologize. Grant used to pretend he was sleeping when I'd start talking about work. Most people just aren't interested, but I'm fascinated by solving problems."

"So, you went to school?"

Olivia nodded. "Community college. I did another semester after I'd started at the bank, online classes, to get my B.S., but then got pregnant with Ezra."

"Do you ever want to go back? And finish it, I mean?"

"Of course I'd love to, but right now? It just doesn't make sense. There's not enough time."

Gracie nodded, then went quiet. They sat in silence as one of the older men who'd been playing cards stood up and let out a hearty laugh, leaning back as he did so, while patting his friend on the shoulder. Gracie and Olivia exchanged a look, both smiling themselves.

"Just how you remember it?" Olivia asked.

"Just about."

"This place is the same. Most of Glenwood is…" Olivia took another drink, then tapped her bright pink nails on the table. Gracie wondered if she'd gotten them done at Lois' Salon recently. Was Lois even still around?

"Have you talked to Hannah?"

Gracie shook her head, letting her hair fall in front of her face, unintentionally hiding behind it. "I haven't, no. I told her when I thought I'd be in, and that I'd have to get a

little sleep before I headed over, so she's not expecting to
see me until tonight. You know, I haven't been back, even
since Cayla was born. I don't know how it will be to see
her."

Olivia looked sympathetic. "Well, she's your sister. You
two were close, weren't you?"

"We were, but that was a long time ago," Gracie said,
fiddling with her bottle cap.

"It was for you and me, too, but I've never been so
happy to see you."

Gracie smiled. "But, you're you."

"What's that supposed to mean?"

"It's nothing bad. You just don't hold a grudge. At least,
I've never known you to."

"I see. That explains why you called me first, then."

Gracie lifted an eyebrow. "You mean before Hannah?"

Olivia met her eyes. "Well, Hannah, and Finn."

The other portion of their conversation that Gracie had
tried to rehearse.

"Well, I haven't talked to Finn in that long, either."

"I know." Olivia looked down at her drink as if
contemplating her next words. "He was real messed up
after you left, ya know. It took him a long time to move
on."

Gracie's cheeks flushed, and she felt her neck growing
warmer by the second. "I know you might not believe me,
Olivia, but it was for the best."

"I know you wouldn't do anything to deliberately hurt
him. I guess I just wish there would have been more
closure for him."

"I left. Isn't that closure enough?"

"I think he always hoped you'd come back."

Of course Finn would think that. He, like Olivia, had
always been a hopeless romantic with a dream.

"He wouldn't have been happy if I'd stayed."

"How do you know?" Olivia asked. "I'm not trying to be rude. I'm just curious."

When Gracie didn't answer, Olivia looked away.

"I'm sorry, Olivia." She wanted to reveal all, but it wouldn't change anything now. Her old friend took another drink.

"I know you are," she said, finally. "Listen, anything you need while you're here, just ask. We'll be at the funeral, too."

"Thank you."

"I'd better get back," Olivia said, reaching for her purse. "And you need to call your sister."

"It's next on my to-do list."

"Good." They climbed out of the booth. Olivia leaned in, hugging her this time much harder. "Call Finn, too. He'll go crazy if you were back and he didn't know. And he'll go even crazier if he finds out I knew and didn't tell him. At least do it for me."

Gracie nodded. "I will."

She stood, watching Olivia leave, unable to move herself. As soon as she'd passed the "Welcome to Glenwood" sign earlier that morning, she'd felt something stirring deep inside, a wistful feeling that she'd been unable to shake. That feeling persisted, growing and tugging on her heart—pulling her closer to her roots, her history and herself.

2.

THE SUN WAS LOWER IN THE SKY, BUT THE HEAT STILL intense as Gracie unlocked her car and climbed in, immediately blasting the air conditioning and letting the cold air unstick the hair from the back of her neck. Sitting back, she swept her hair up, twisting it up for a moment of relief from the sweaty, stringy mess of tangled tresses, before letting it fall back down. As she dug into her purse for her phone, it occurred to her that it wasn't just the heat overwhelming her.

When Hannah had called to tell her of their mother's passing, she'd been somber. The conversation had been strained. It was the first time they'd spoken in over a year. Hannah hadn't even said hi when Gracie had answered the phone.

"Mom's dead," she'd whispered, barely audible.

"I'll be right there," Gracie had said, her own voice a whisper as well.

"Do you want to stay here?" Hannah asked.

"I'll get a room. I'm not sure when I'll get in. I'll call you when I do."

"Okay." Hannah had said, before breaking through the following silence with her soft crying.

"It'll be okay, H."

"Just get here soon, yeah?" Hannah had hung up before Gracie had been able to respond. It had hit Gracie then, just how much distance had grown between her and her sister. When they were young kids, Hannah had been the quieter one. But as they grew up, something changed. With each passing year, Hannah's boldness took flight, and she quickly found her voice. Meanwhile, Gracie had more and more trouble with hers.

Not only was Hannah the opinionated eldest sibling, she was also a brainiac. All through school she had flown through assignments that should have been difficult, solving physics equations in half the time that it took her classmates. Even when they were younger, Hannah always caught on quickly. When Hannah learned to ride her bike, it took her exactly three tries to master it. When Gracie tried two years later to do the same, she was still unable to do it after three days. At the time it had infuriated her. She remembered crying to her father about it one night. He had shrugged it—or maybe more accurately, her—off. "You know," he'd said, in a voice with a hint of condescension. "Everyone's got different gifts. Your sister's just blessed with many."

Gracie had returned to her room after that, defeated. It was Hannah who had come to her aid, helping her through the last of her homework.

"Thanks H," she'd said as her sister got up to leave. Hannah had turned around and put her hands on her hips.

"You don't listen to Daddy, you hear?"

She'd stared at her older sibling, unsure of what to say. Hannah had sighed melodramatically, then come back to sit beside Gracie on the bed.

"He doesn't have any idea what he's talking about," she'd said, patting her little sister on the knee. "You're special, Gracie. I mean, you understand things."

Gracie had shrugged, chewing on the end of her pencil. "I never understand any of this stuff."

Hannah shook her head, frustrated. "That's not what I mean. I'm not talking about this stuff, school or whatever. I'm talking about the world. You have a sense about things—about people. You know them, just by watching 'em for a few minutes. It's like you're in tune with everyone you meet."

She'd watched Hannah as she spoke, trying to make sense of her words.

"Remember when we ran into Miss Maycee with Mama a few weeks back?"

Gracie shook her head.

"And Mama kept asking her how you were doing in her class, and they were talkin' just like nothin'. You remember?"

"Yeah, H, I remember."

"And then right before we turned to go, you went up and whispered something in her ear and gave her a hug?"

"Mm-hmmm."

"And what did you say you said to her?"

"I told you already. I just told her she reminded me of Audrey Hepburn. So elegant. Just like a movie star."

"That's right, and she got the biggest smile on her face."

"So?"

"So, what you didn't know was that she called Mama later that day, going on about what a terrible morning she'd had. That she'd overslept, gotten into a fight with one of her kids, found the dog dead on the back deck—he was old, but it was still unexpected—just a bunch of things had gone wrong. And then you said a few nice words to her, and she smiled. I'm pretty sure Mama came to the conclusion that she'd been a hair's breadth away from drowning her sorrows in a bottle of whiskey."

Gracie stared at her, stupefied. At the time, she wasn't sure what drowning your sorrows meant, but she knew what whiskey did to people. She'd seen the effects on her daddy. "But that was just chance, H."

"It wasn't. It's happened lots of times." Hannah got up from the bed, trying to brush out the wrinkles in her dress. "Just promise you won't let anybody tell you you're not amazing."

Gracie shrugged. "Okay. I promise."

"I mean it, Gracie Mae. I'm serious. I saw your face after you talked to Daddy."

Frowning, Gracie replied, "You know you're his favorite."

Hannah had turned on her heels then and walked out of the room, but Gracie heard her voice down the hallway. "I know no such thing."

Oh, Hannah. Her dear older sister. How could she have let so much time pass without ever checking in? She yearned for that closeness they once shared, especially now that their mother was gone.

Hannah's phone call had come after a quick email exchange, where Gracie had finally relinquished her phone number after receiving an email with the subject line *Emergency*. After the call, Gracie had stood, phone in hand, as memories of her mother flooded back— memories she hadn't thought about in years, things she'd tried to forget in order to make a new life for herself. Mama laughing as she frosted pink cupcakes for Hannah's eighth birthday. Her freckles popping out across her nose as she swayed back and forth on their old porch swing. The last time Gracie had seen her, the night before she left Glenwood, Gracie had sworn Mama knew something, but she never gave it away if she did. She'd walked back from Finn's, her mind racing and holding back tears, to find Mama there waiting for her. Gracie had often wondered how she'd known Gracie would be there. And whether she knew that her embrace had been the only thing holding Gracie up the rest of the way home.

When they'd made it back, her mother had turned to her. "I love you, Gracie Girl."

"I know, Mama."

"Some days have been hard. I'm sure you've noticed. And I'm sorry I haven't always been able to be here in the moment with you. Workin' two jobs since your father left, well, it hasn't given me much choice. But, you know, whatever happens in this life, I've loved you. You carry that with you always."

Gracie had nodded as her mother had embraced her once more before going into the house. Gracie hadn't seen her mama since.

Now, she was finally back in Glenwood, and it was too late to tell her mother all the things she should have said that day.

Back at the hotel, she realized she'd forgotten to take her key with her, and would have to get another. There was a new front desk clerk, too busy with his phone to greet her as she entered. He hurriedly got her a new key, then went back to it. Gracie thanked him anyway, then turned to leave, nearly bumping into the person behind her.

"I'm sorry, I didn't hear anyone..." she said. She was about to apologize again when she finally noticed the face of the stranger.

"Hello, Gracie."

She would have known his face anywhere, but it had changed, too. His eyes, once a deep blue, now looked lighter, almost gray. Could eye color change like that?

"Finn." His name on her lips was a strange sensation after so much time. She breathed in, uneasy.

"You don't sound too happy to see me," he said.

"Just surprised is all." Had Olivia called him after all? That quickly?

"Grant let it slip you were in town," he said, reading her mind.

"It's been a long time," she said, unable to take her eyes off of him.

"It has."

"Forgot my key," she said, holding it up between them.

"So I see." His face was serious, and he was studying her. She couldn't quite catch her breath. Of all the reunion scenarios that had run through her head over the past 24 hours, this had not been one of them. "Walk with me?"

She nodded, following him out the door and back into the heat. They rounded the building and began to walk, taking a sidewalk past the apartment complex next door to the small park on the other side. Two teenage boys were shooting hoops nearby and a mother was pushing a toddler in one of the swings.

"I'm sorry to hear about your mother," Finn said as they turned up a pathway leading into the park.

"Thank you." Gracie looked up at him, but he was looking ahead. They came to a picnic table and Finn sat down, facing Gracie. She stood, awkwardly, fidgeting with her fingers.

"So, where've you been, Gracie?" he asked, finally. She looked up, meeting his eyes. His features had drawn together, making him look too serious for their airy summer surroundings.

When she didn't answer right away, he shook his head slowly back and forth.

"You know, you look the same. I can't believe it, but you look just like I remember."

"Do I?" she asked. She didn't feel the same. "You look different. I mean, look at you. You're in a suit."

"Speaking of," he said, pulling on the arm of his jacket. "It's hot out here." He pulled out his other arm, then rolled the sleeves of his dress shirt up and loosened his tie. "I left straight from work after Grant called me."

"What for? I would have called you." The words slipped out in a clipped tone. She surprised herself, sounding so cold.

"Would you?"

She could tell by his face that he didn't believe her.

"I would. I promised Olivia I would."

"That's the only reason?"

"No," she said. She felt defensive when she didn't have anything to defend.

He was quiet, staring at her. She looked at the ground.

"You want to sit?" he asked.

"I'm alright."

He shrugged, obviously hurt that she was so standoffish. "So, where are you living now?" he asked.

"Pomroy. It's about seven hours from here."

"I know it."

"I went to school there—just finished last year." She turned around, walking a few paces to a grassy spot, then slipped off her shoes and sat down, letting the sun hit her skin. Working nights, she usually slept during the day. Her skin was white, and she knew she could easily burn. Her shoulders were already turning pink from the walk from the hotel, but it felt good, basking in the sun's rays.

"And what do you do now?" he asked.

"I'm a nurse," she said. It was the one thing in her life she was most proud of, putting herself through school so she could do something that really mattered. Working with the children at the hospital gave her life meaning, and she felt grateful that she had that now, after searching for it before in all the wrong places.

"That's great," Finn said, watching her.

"So, what about you?" Gracie asked.

"Well, after I graduated, I moved over to Ashland and started doing real estate. It's been a lucrative career, and I've been lucky, but I've worked hard for it, too." He leaned over to untie his shoes, slipping them off along with his argyle socks. "I like seeing my clients find the right place. It makes me happy knowing that I'm helping them create a home." He stood from the picnic table and sat beside her on the grass, wiggling his toes as a short-lived breeze brought relief from the heat. "Have you seen Hannah yet?"

Gracie shook her head. "No," Gracie said, watching as he leaned back on his elbows. "Have you seen her lately?"

"I make it back here pretty often. Grant and Olivia don't want me becoming a stranger, and they want the boys to know me. I've run into Hannah a few times. The last time was probably two months ago."

"So you've met Cayla?"

"I have. She's a beautiful girl, Gracie. Sassy, too. I think she keeps Hannah on her toes."

Gracie smiled at that. "Well, it wouldn't take much to do that. Hannah's so by the book."

"I think you'd be surprised. A few years back I saw your sister out in Ashland. She was with some friends, out dancing. I've never seen anyone bust a move like that aside from you."

"Hannah was in a club?" That was not the Hannah she had known.

"I'm sure it was just one of those rare Mom's Night Out kind of things."

Gracie shook her head in disbelief. "It's hard for me to imagine it."

Finn sat up and turned to face her. "I know you're not ready to say why you left, but why didn't you come back?" he asked.

"I just couldn't," she said as the two teenagers passed by them, dribbling their basketballs as they went. "Things changed, and the longer I was away, the harder it was to face everyone. It was easier to start fresh. For a while, it was the only way I could keep going."

"But why?"

She felt her heart skip a beat. "Is that so important? It doesn't change anything now."

That hit a nerve. She saw his entire body tense, and he jumped up, walking away from her before whipping around again. "Dammit, Gracie." His voice boomed over her. "Who are you?"

She didn't respond. How could she, without telling him the one thing she didn't tell anyone.

"Why won't you talk to me? It's been ten years, for God's sake. You haven't been back once in all this time… and now you show up and…you're you, but you're not. I want to be here for you. I want to help you." His voice softened, his tone kind. Even so, Gracie couldn't help but feel exposed. "Tell me how."

"I can't," she said, standing up so they were on equal ground, but it didn't give her the self-assurance she thought it would. "I have to go."

"Fine," he responded, turning his face away. "Go."

"Finn…"

"Just go."

Once she was back in her car, she started driving south. She'd been close to telling him everything. She'd wanted to. She'd forgotten the magnetic pull between them. He was the person she'd always felt closest to in the world. Outside of her parents and older sister, he was the only other one who knew her so completely. They'd grown up together, born just a few months apart, running around their neighborhood like wild things.

At the four-way stop, she turned left, driving past cornfields, making her way to the winding road that would take her to her destination.

A moment later she was rapping on a large wooden door. When it opened, she sighed in relief.

"Gracie?"

"Hi, Hannah," she said, stepping forward to hug her sister.

The older Brannen girl stepped back, holding the door open for her. "What are you doing here? I thought you were going to call first."

Gracie stepped into the house. It was small, but Hannah didn't have a lot, so it didn't look too small. It definitely wasn't cluttered. Everything had its place, and the items that were displayed around the rooms were put there purposefully. They had a reason for being there, which was more than Gracie could say for herself at the moment.

"I figured I'd try my luck. See if you were home."

"C'mon in. Cayla's still at camp. She should be back any minute."

She followed Hannah into the kitchen where she was waiting for some banana bread to come out of the oven. "Mom's recipe. Remember?" Gracie nodded. Of course she did. They'd had it at least once a week growing up.

"How is Cayla?" Gracie asked, parking herself on the bar stool next to the counter.

"Growing like a weed. She's six now. Can you believe it?"

"I can't." The fact that her sister had had a baby and that Gracie had never met her, was hard to swallow. They'd been close once. Closer than a lot of sisters. But now, here they sat, virtual strangers. She owed her sister more than that. "I'm sorry, H."

Her sister looked up at her words. "I appreciate that, Gracie."

"I never meant for things to go this way."

Hannah crossed her arms in front of her, scowling. "Well, they did."

Gracie sighed, not wanting to say the wrong thing. "And I'm sorry for that."

"Does that mean you'll be coming back around again? I mean, is this a one-time visit or are you back?"

"Well, I'm not back, like, permanently, but I suppose I'm hoping we can salvage what's left of our relationship."

She saw Hannah's shoulders drop just as the timer went off on the oven. She turned, slipping on two oven mitts that featured little yellow kittens in Santa hats, and Gracie smiled at the sight of them being used in the middle of summer. When Hannah pulled out the bread, the delicious aroma became even stronger, seeping into the kitchen, causing Gracie's stomach to rumble. Hannah set the pan down, then slipped off the mitts.

"This is just a lot to think about right now," Hannah said as she fanned the bread with one hand, avoiding Gracie's eyes.

"Hannah, look at me," she whispered.

Hannah dropped her hand to her side and she slowly turned toward her sister. "I'm not mad," she said.

"I'd understand if you were."

"Oh, Gracie," she said, turning around once she'd plopped the mitts on the counter. "We'll always have a relationship, whether I see you every ten years or every day. You're my sister. I have no idea why you haven't been back, and yes, it's hurtful that this will be the first time you meet my daughter, but we're family, and at this point we're all each other has."

Gracie was at a loss for words, but she finally choked out a few. "I don't deserve you."

"Yes, you do," Hannah said, cautious in her delivery of the words. She glanced back at the banana bread as if she were smelling the scent and Gracie thought how much she reminded her of their mother in that moment. When she turned her head back, she was all business, as if it was time for her to finish a task on her to-do list. "Now, come over here and let me have a good look at you," she said.

Gracie stood up, her tangled hair had gone even more awry, while her face was streaked from earlier sweat that had dried to her cheeks when she'd entered the air-conditioned house. She wasn't much to look at, but Hannah pulled her in, embracing her.

"I did shower today, you know..." Gracie began, feeling self-conscious.

"You look amazing. I've been waiting for this day for a long time. If I'm not going to let some petty anger get in the way of it, why would I let a little sweat?" She let out a chuckle, then turned back into the kitchen. "Would you like a piece of this banana bread?"

"Sure," Gracie said, a little too quickly.

Hannah smiled. "I heard your stomach earlier. How long has it been since you last ate?"

"I grabbed something on the drive—about halfway through."

"Well, you must be starving!"

Gracie was about to argue, but that bread was calling to her, pushing her to remember, to face the things she'd run from, the people she'd left behind. Hannah set a plate in front of her and she took a bite, the homemade goodness rich and familiar and fine.

Hannah walked ahead of her, humming one of the hymns they'd just heard at church. She walked in a straight line, while Gracie zigzagged back and forth behind her.

"What'd you ask for for your birthday this year?" Hannah asked, turning her head to look at Gracie as she continued to walk along the creek.

"Nothin'."

"What do you mean nothin'?"

"You heard me. Nothin'. Mama and Daddy can't afford it."

"How do you know?" Hannah stopped walking.

"I heard 'em fighting about money again."

Hannah considered this. "Has either of 'em asked you?"

"What I want?"

"Yeah. Has Mama asked you about it yet?"

"Nah. I don't want them to, either. You keep your yap shut about it, will ya?"

"But, Gracie, your birthday's next week!"

Hannah always cared too much about birthdays. In Gracie's opinion they just caused trouble. No adults that she knew liked their birthdays, especially not their father, who wouldn't even tell anyone when it was. In fact, the only person she knew that did like them was Hannah.

"Finn asked me about Daddy today," Gracie said, changing the subject.

She saw a flash of anger in Hannah's eyes after she said it, but when her sister replied, she kept her voice calm. "What'd he say?"

"He was goin' on about seeing him and Kit. They were coming out of some seedy place, Finn said. He said his own daddy turned him away and hurried him back into the car, but he looked back and saw two ladies with 'em."

"You gonna believe everything Finn tells you?"

"Why not? He's known us since we were born!"

"Not me. I'm two years older than both of you."

Gracie rolled her eyes. "You think because you're double digits now you're some big hotshot, but Finn and I are the ones that know everything."

"You just know small-town gossip, and that's not ever gonna do you any good, Gracie Mae."

The girls walked on in silence. Gracie hated how young she always felt around Hannah. She thought for sure this tidbit of information would have Hannah in hysterics or, at the very least, storming back home to confront their father. She should've known better. Hannah wouldn't do anything to rock the boat, which meant it was left to her to stand up for their mother.

"You think Mama knows?" Gracie asked a while later, as they set up a picnic. Hannah spread out a blanket and plopped down on it. She stared at the water, but her eyes told Gracie she was far off, someplace else. "H?" she repeated.

"Quit your worryin' now." Hannah said. "Let's enjoy our lunch. Mama packed PB&J and some of her banana bread, too."

Gracie crossed her arms in front of her. "Aren't you going to answer me?"

"I don't know if Mama knows, but if she does, she'll handle it how she wants. It's not our place to get involved."

"Like hell it ain't," Gracie said, flabbergasted. "That's our Mama."

Hannah's lips pursed and her brow furrowed. "You listen to me, Gracie. Stay out of it, ya hear? It's not our place." Hannah reached into their basket again. "Here, eat your sandwich, then we'll go stick our feet in the water for a bit."

Gracie took a bite, letting the peanut butter stick to the roof of her mouth.

"You promise?" Hannah asked, eyeing her.

"Promise what?"

"To keep your dang mouth shut, that's what."

"Yeah, fine. I promise."

It wasn't until years later that Gracie realized what she'd missed that day. And why Hannah had made her make such a promise.

The door opened, and Cayla bounded in, followed by Dave. Gracie's heart stopped. The girl was beautiful, and it took her breath away. When Cayla saw her, she stopped suddenly and shyly hid behind Hannah.

Gracie knelt down, trying to meet her niece's eyes. "Cayla." She breathed out the name, overcome with emotion. "I'm your Aunt Gracie."

Cayla peeked out, her big brown eyes full of curiosity.

Hannah put an arm around her daughter. "Aunt Gracie is my sister, Cayla. You remember?" She glanced at Gracie. "She's seen pictures of you."

Slowly, Cayla emerged, stepping carefully toward Gracie.

"I'm so happy to meet you," Gracie said, wanting to pull the girl to her and hug her tightly. She refrained, keeping her distance as Cayla studied her.

When she spoke, her voice flowed into Gracie's ears like the sweet song of the Cerulean Warbler, a bird she and Hannah had listened for whenever they found themselves tromping through the wooded areas around their house. It was a high-pitched sound, clear and delicate. "Aunt Gracie?" Her mouth gaped open.

Gracie nodded. "Hi," she said, pushing her own emotions down so she could focus on the small figure in front of her.

The girl came closer, extending a hand to her cheek. "I know you," she said, her face breaking into a smile. "Mommy!" she yelled, turning back to Hannah. "It's Aunt Gracie!"

Hannah laughed. "I know. I know. Isn't it wonderful?"

Dave walked through the door then, and Cayla shouted at him, too. "Daddy! It's Aunt Gracie!" She danced around the room, her arms flailing about. She had the energy of a Jack Russell pup.

"So I see," he said, extending his hand to the sister-in-law he'd never met. "It's so nice to meet you."

His sandy blonde hair was short, a buzz cut, and Gracie wondered if he'd cut it that way for summer or if he always wore it like that. Gracie took his hand in hers. "It's nice to meet you as well." She smiled, unsure of what to do next. Cayla watched them expectantly.

"Cayla, why don't we go unpack your backpack? We'll let Mommy and Aunt Gracie finish talking and then we'll all go into town to get some dinner."

"Do I have to?" Cayla asked, frowning. She was looking up at Hannah.

"Yes. Go with Daddy." Hannah's eyebrows arched, and she momentarily stood, unflinching, in the silent battle of wills with her daughter.

"Oh, alright." Cayla stamped out of the kitchen and down the hallway, followed by Dave.

The two women watched them go before Gracie reacted. "H, she's amazing."

Hannah smiled, a look of pure pride on her face. "She is something."

"You're a mom. A good one, too, I'm sure."

"Just like ours was," Hannah replied, a hint of sadness in her voice.

"She was, wasn't she?" Gracie couldn't shake her guilt, and it weighed on her. She felt dizzy.

"Is that okay? If we go out to dinner?"

"We don't have to on my account," Gracie said. "And you made that wonderful banana bread."

"Oh, it'll keep. And it'll be good for us to get out of the house. There's been a lot of sadness here lately. I'm glad Cayla has something to take her mind off her grandma for a bit."

"Sure. How is she doing with Mama's passing?"

"You know, she's doing alright. I know she understands what happened, but it's hard to see her become emotional. You know, I'd do anything to make sure she never felt any pain."

Gracie didn't say anything. Hannah didn't know it, but she kept saying just the thing to make Gracie feel worse. Her mother had probably felt that way about her, and she'd left, indefinitely. Forever, maybe, as far as her mother was concerned. She'd probably been hoping at the end she'd see her one last time. Gracie didn't know how she'd forgive herself.

When she looked up, Hannah was watching her. "Mama knew you loved her, Gracie."

Suddenly, tears welled up in her eyes. "Did she?"

Hannah nodded, taking a step closer to Gracie and wiping away a tear that had begun sliding down her cheek. "A mama knows these things."

And Gracie knew it was true.

3.

"Pizza! Pizza!" Cayla yelled from beside Gracie in the back seat. Dave had just asked what Gracie felt like for dinner, and Cayla had answered for her.

Hannah turned around from the front seat, shushing her daughter. "Cayla, Aunt Gracie is going to choose tonight."

Cayla leaned over to Gracie, putting a hand up to cover her mouth and whispered, "Say pizza, Aunt Gracie. Daddy'll take us to Antonio's. They have the best pizza in town!" She was giddy, reminding Gracie of herself as a kid.

She winked at Cayla, then said, "How about Antonio's?"

Hannah rolled her eyes, then turned back to the front. "I give up. I am destined to have pizza every time we go out to eat."

"Don't worry," Dave said, taking hold of his wife's hand. "I'll take you out, just us, one of these nights and we'll go wherever you want."

It made Gracie's heart stop, hearing how lovingly he spoke to Hannah. All these years, Gracie had wondered if she had married someone like their daddy. As it turned out, Dave was the complete opposite of their dear old dad.

"What kind of pizza do you like?" Gracie asked Cayla, who was now reaching for the button to roll her window down. She pushed it in, sticking her face as close to it as she could from her booster seat, before turning to Gracie with a big smile on her face.

"Cheese."

"Just cheese?"

Cayla nodded.

"No pepperoni?"

Cayla made a face, sticking out her tongue.

"What?" Gracie asked. What kid didn't like pepperoni pizza? "How about sausage?" Cayla shook her head. "Marshmallow?" Her niece laughed at that.

"No such thing," she said.

"Oh yes there is," Gracie said, pointing toward the front seat. "Just ask your mom."

Cayla's eyes grew wide. "Mama! Gracie said there's marshmallow pizza. Is that true?"

Hannah turned around again, shooting Gracie a look. She didn't respond, which was enough for Cayla.

"Can we have it? Oh pretty, pretty please? Can we?"

"I don't think Antonio's has it, honey. Aunt Gracie and I used to make it as kids."

Cayla crossed her arms in front of her and stuck out her bottom lip, causing Gracie to laugh out loud.

"I'm sorry," she whispered. "I shouldn't have said anything." Cayla's frown retreated, but her arms stayed put, not relenting yet. "How about this? I'll go shopping and get all the ingredients for marshmallow pizza and we'll make it before I go home, okay?"

Cayla contemplated this. "When are you going home?"

Gracie wasn't even sure. She had intended to go straight back after the funeral, but she kept being surprised by her old life, the one that, in some ways, had moved right along without her. "I'm not exactly sure, but not for a few more days. Plenty of time to load up on marshmallow-y goodness."

Cayla smiled, uncrossing her arms and leaning toward Gracie. "I'm so happy you're here, Aunt Gracie," she whispered.

Gracie smiled. "Me too, Cayla."

When they'd stuffed themselves with pizza and returned to Dave and Hannah's, Gracie found herself sitting on the living room floor with 20 barrettes of different colors all over her head.

"Aunt Gracie, you have beautiful hair," Cayla said, clipping a blue bow into her hair.

"Thank you."

"It looks just like Princess Belle." The little girl rifled through her bag of barrettes, looking for something else to add to her creation.

"Is she your favorite princess?"

"No, Sleeping Beauty is my favorite." Ah, the princess with the pink dress, Gracie thought.

"Well, you have hair just like her," Gracie said. Cayla nodded, still concentrating on the task at hand.

"And you and Mama have the same as Belle." Cayla said. "Someday I'll have the same as Belle, too." She was probably right. It didn't look like Cayla had Dave's coloring, and Hannah's had turned brown the same as Gracie's had.

"Alright, Cayla," Hannah said as she came into the room. "It's bedtime. Daddy'll tuck you in and read you a story."

"Can't Aunt Gracie?"

"Not tonight," Hannah said. Cayla was about to object when Hannah gave her "the look" again. "I want to talk with your Aunt Gracie for a bit. You know it's been a long time since I've seen her, too."

Resigned to the fact that she wouldn't change her mother's mind, she turned to Dave, who had followed Hannah into the room. "How about two books, Daddy?" Cayla asked, giving her negotiation skills a go.

"Oh, alright. I suppose," he said, sighing, but looking pleased that this would help get her off to bed.

"Did you hear that Mama? Daddy is going to read me two books!"

"I heard." Hannah reached down and hugged her daughter. "I love you, munchkin."

"Princess Cayla, Mama."

"I love you, Princess Cayla." She kissed her nose, and Cayla smiled.

"I love you, Queen Mama." She turned to look at Gracie. "I love you, Princess Gracie."

"Isn't Gracie a queen, too?" Hannah asked, winking at Gracie.

Cayla shook her head. "There's only one queen, and besides I want Gracie to be a princess like me."

"I would love to be a princess like you." Gracie said, leaning forward to hug Cayla. "I love you, Princess Cayla," she whispered. "Sleep tight. Don't let the bed bugs bite."

Cayla giggled, then skipped down the hall. "What are bed bugs, Daddy?" they heard her ask Dave before he closed the door.

"Oops. I didn't think about that before I said it."

Hannah shrugged. "Six-year-olds are inquisitive, huh?"

Gracie laughed. "They sure are."

"You want to go sit on the porch?" Hannah asked.

"Sure, just let me get these bows out." Gracie reached up and pulled them from her hair, letting her bangs, which Cayla had pulled back and clasped into one extra-large bow, spring free.

They moved through the house to the back porch. As soon as she stepped outside, Gracie could hear the sounds of summer. She spotted a katydid as soon as she entered as it finished its chorus of "ch-ch-ch." The little green body was silent for less than a second, then started back in.

"The katydids are out in droves about now," Hannah said. "They just love the lights there." She pointed to the three lights hanging from the gable porch roof.

"It's nice now that the sun's down," Gracie said. She sat in a rocking chair a few steps from the door, while

Hannah sat down on the porch steps, leaning against the white post behind her.

"I love sitting out here in the summer," Hannah said. After a while, she lifted her head and looked at Gracie. "I'm so glad you're here."

"Me too, H."

"I know you've got a whole other life waiting for you back home, but it feels right having you back."

The katydid's song ended again, and Gracie took a deep breath.

"I wish I could take a million things back," she said, her voice soft and full of emotion.

"Don't wish that," Hannah said. "It's water under the bridge. I just hope you're happy." When Gracie didn't respond, Hannah prodded her. "Are you?"

"I suppose I am."

"That doesn't sound too convincing."

Gracie didn't know what else to say. She was happy in her job. She'd never been happier, in that regard. But she still felt as though something was missing. And that something seemed to be creeping up on her the longer she was in Glenwood.

"How did you and Dave meet?" she asked after a while.

Hannah smiled. "Mama introduced us."

"Yeah?"

Her sister nodded. "It was while she was working at the credit union, the one off our old street."

"Is that the one Olivia worked at?"

"No, she was at Bank of Glenwood." Hannah stretched her legs across the top step, moving her right ankle in a circular motion as if she was trying to get a kink out. "Anyway, he was about to take his lunch break when Mama tripped through the front door, spilling her purse open. Everything went flying, including her wallet, which had a picture of me riding Timber in it. You remember him?" She paused, recalling the details of the story. "Gosh, it's been years since I've been riding. Anyway, he spotted it as he was helping her pick up all her belongings, and she saw him staring at it. She asked if he'd fancy taking me out to dinner and that was that."

"You went on a blind date?" Gracie asked, surprised.

"Well, I trusted Mama. And, to be honest, I hadn't had a lot of luck meeting any men. It seemed for a while I was getting nowhere fast with immature boys."

Gracie nodded.

"What about you? Seeing anyone?"

"No," she said. Her mind went to Walt, who she'd dated for almost a year before she went back to nursing school. "I saw this guy for a while, but it didn't pan out. We were friends, more so than boyfriend and girlfriend."

"So it wasn't serious?"

"It probably was for a while, but he wanted things to move forward." She hesitated. "I wasn't ready."

"I don't suppose you're ready now?"

Gracie laughed, letting the sound echo around the porch. "Why? You know somebody?"

Hannah chuckled. "The only people I know are parents from Cayla's school and Dave. And he's taken."

"Dave's a good one, H."

"Thanks. I think so."

"Have you seen much of Finn?" Gracie asked. She had wanted to be less obvious when she asked about Finn, but there was no way to do that with Hannah.

"Not a lot. You know he comes up to visit every now and then."

"Olivia said he's doing pretty well in Ashland."

"He is," Hannah said. "You know I saw a billboard with his face on it the other day?"

"What?"

"Yeah, Cayla and I were driving to the city for an appointment and I about crashed into the car in front of me when I saw his big cheeky grin staring back at me."

"Now that I've got to see."

Hannah smiled, then stood up. "I'm going in for a glass of water. You want one?"

"Sure."

Her sister moved to the front door, but before she opened it she turned back to Gracie. "I don't think he's seeing anyone, Gracie."

"What makes you say that?" Gracie asked.

She shrugged, and walked inside.

Gracie leaned her head back, moving her chair back and forth as she listened to the katydid, its song never-ending, as if singing her home.

4.

"FINN, WAIT UP, YOU WANKER!" GRACIE RAN BAREFOOT through the grass, her feet covered in dirt and grime. She slowed down, standing on her toes to go over the gravel road.

"Keep up, Gracie. Riley's waitin' for us. We gotta hurry."

"Who cares about Riley? He's a wanker, too." Gracie disliked Riley Walker more than anyone else in their class. He'd pulled her skirt up on the first day of school—a skirt she hadn't even wanted to wear in the first place. "Why you hangin' out with Riley anyhow?"

"I'm not. He was just braggin' to everybody about it on the way to school. And stop saying wanker. You don't even know what it means."

"I do, too," Gracie argued.

"What's it mean, then?"

"I'm not tellin' you."

Finn laughed. "Girls shouldn't be goin' around sayin' wanker."

"Girls can say anything boys can." Gracie crossed her arms in front of her, defiantly.

"Can we talk about this another time? We hafta go."

Finn started running again, and Gracie watched him go before resigning herself to the fact that she needed to keep up if she wanted to tag along, which is exactly what she was doing. Finn had told her as much when he spied her following him through the fields in their backyards.

Gracie caught up just as Finn slowed down near a large gray barn, looking around.

"Over here," he whispered, waving his hand for Gracie to follow him.

They crept into the barn, which had part of its roof torn off or blown in. There were no pieces around that Gracie could see, so it must've blown off somewhere.

"What are we doing here, Finn?" Gracie whispered back.

"I told you. We're meeting Riley."

She followed Finn closely. The sun came in through the open hole in the roof and the door behind them, but otherwise the barn was dark.

"Hey, Finn," they heard from further inside the barn.

"Riley?" Finn's voice startled Gracie. "Where are you?"

"Up here," They both looked across the barn, where they saw Riley at the top of a ladder, leading up to a second-story loft. "Why'd you bring her with you?"

"What're you doin' up there, you wanker?" Gracie yelled. Finn shot her a look, but she just shrugged.

"Come over and see for yourself," Riley yelled back. "That is, if you're not scared."

They walked to the ladder and Finn grabbed the bottom of the ladder. Just as he put his foot up to climb, he stopped. "You go on up first, Gracie."

"Huh?" she asked, her eyes moving from Riley's figure above back to Finn.

"You go first. I'll come up after."

"Why?"

"What do you mean why? Just go."

"Is this some kind of trick?"

"No, it ain't."

"Then why do I hafta go first?"

Finn rolled his eyes. "In case you fall."

Gracie made a face. "You think you're gonna catch me, then?"

"I could catch you if I needed to."

"You couldn't even catch a baby kitten with those scrawny arms."

"Ah, Gracie. Just go. C'mon, I'm lettin' you tag along, aren't I?"

Tag along. There were those dreaded words again. Her father always said them to Hannah when he wanted her to get Gracie out of the house. "Why don't you let Gracie here tag along?" he'd say.

"Are you guys comin' or what?" Riley called down.

Finn was still waiting for her to climb. "Fine," she said, finally, puffing out her chest as she let her breath out.

Finn smiled, clearly pleased about getting his way.

When they'd made it to the top, Gracie brushed off her hands and looked around. "So, now what?" she asked, turning to Riley.

"What do you mean?" Riley asked.

"What's the cool thing we're seeing?"

Riley rolled his eyes. "You're seeing it."

"A few old boards and two bales of hay?" she laughed. "This is why we came all the way out here?"

"This place is cool," Riley shot back, clearly offended.

"A dumb old barn?"

"Nobody asked you," Riley said.

"Gracie, knock it off," Finn said. "What else were you gonna do today?" He had a point. Gracie would've just been walking around the neighborhood, bored and itching for something to do. She shut her mouth and motioned like she was zipping it.

"Besides," Riley said, walking over to where the roof was blown off. "I heard there was a murder here."

Gracie's heart stopped. "You did not!"

- 41 -

"Did too. Dillon said so after I told him I found this place. He said no one lives on this farm anymore because someone was murdered."

"He did, Gracie," Finn agreed. "On our walk to school. He said the old owner had died under mysterious circumstances and now no one wants to live here."

"That doesn't mean he was murdered," Gracie said. "Didn't you ask your parents? They probably know. It's not that far from our neighborhood."

"If I ask them, then they'll wonder why I want to know," Riley said.

"So?" Gracie asked.

"So then I'll have to tell them I've been here." Riley walked to the window, looking down at the small farmhouse and fields below.

A breeze went through the barn and Gracie shuddered. "This place is creepy. C'mon, let's go Finn."

"Just a minute," Finn said, squatting down in the corner of the loft. "There's something over here." Gracie and Riley walked over, joining him in the corner. "It's a switchblade."

"No way!" Riley said. "Let me see it." Finn gave it to Riley, who eyed it like buried treasure. "Maybe this is the murder weapon!"

"If there was a murder here, they would've searched the place already," Finn said. "Somebody probably just left it here."

"Riley, put it down. We shouldn't take it in case they come back." Gracie looked around the barn. She was beginning to feel creeped out by the place.

"No way," Riley said. "Finders keepers."

"Alright, keep it Riley," Finn said. "But let's head back. Gracie looks like she's seen a ghost."

The three of them climbed back down, with Riley putting the blade in his pocket. As they walked out of the barn, Gracie whispered to Finn, "He's gonna tell everyone that's a murder weapon, you know."

Finn smiled. "I know."

"Finn! Finn! Chase me!" Judd yelled, running across the yard, followed closely by his older brother. Ezra's head was cocked back in laughter while he ran—the two brothers looking like crazed animals.

Finn put down the tailgating chairs he was carrying and darted towards them, causing screams and fits of giggles from the two boys.

"Run, Judd!" Ezra yelled, jumping up and down. Judd scurried behind Gracie, grabbing onto her legs. "Save me!" he shouted at Gracie, who reached down and patted his shoulder.

"Don't worry. He won't get you if you're by me." She smiled down at him.

"That's what you think," Finn said, reaching through her legs and grabbing Judd. The boy tried to cling to her leg but Finn scooped him up, throwing him above his head. Judd howled in delight, but still flailed his arms about, trying to escape.

Ezra bounded over as Finn set Judd down on the ground. "He got you good," he said, nudging his younger brother in the shoulder. Judd looked up at Gracie, a frown on his face.

"I thought you were gonna save me!"

Gracie bit her bottom lip, then smiled. "I guess I'm not a very good saver," she said. Finn winked at her.

"I guess not," he replied. He looked up at her, shading his eyes from the sun, still as blaring as it had been earlier in the day. "Who are you?"

"My name's Gracie. I'm a friend of your mom and dad," she said.

"And me," Finn added, ruffling Judd's hair.

"How come we've never seen you before?" Ezra asked, picking up a football at the edge of the yard, then turning to look at her.

Gracie cleared her throat, looking from Judd to Ezra. Both boys looked at her expectantly. She was about to answer them when Olivia stepped out onto the front porch, waving them all in.

"Food's on the grill," she said, smiling. "Boys, why don't you give our guests some space? Dinner's about ready…time to get cleaned up."

"Mama, who is Gracie?" Judd asked, trudging up to his mother.

"She's one of my dearest friends," she answered, shooting Gracie a smile. "Now go on inside and wash your hands. You're filthy, mister."

"I'm not filthy, Mama. I didn't even dig in the mud."

"Well, you look like you did." The boys whined as they made their way back inside, but they went. Olivia turned as Gracie and Finn approached the porch.

"Apple pie?" Gracie asked, holding it up.

"You made that?" Olivia looked impressed.

"Well, I can't say I did it all on my own. Cayla helped and Hannah supervised."

"It looks delicious." Olivia took the pie and held open the door for them. "Grant's out back manning the grill. Burgers and hot dogs alright?"

"Sounds perfect," Finn said, taking hold of the door for Olivia. Relieved, she entered her house with Gracie on her heels. Gracie looked around the house in awe. While from the outside it looked like a typical farm house, the inside had been done up to look like something you would have seen in downtown Ashland. The modern furniture, updated countertops and brightly painted walls were straight out of a magazine.

"Olivia, your home is beautiful," she said, trying not to stare.

"Thank you," she replied, beaming. "I'm a DIY-er. Everything here's been done by me, cheapest I could do it. We bought this house right after we got married so we've had years to make it into a home. It didn't look like this at the start."

"I can attest to that," Finn said. "Remember that old refrigerator we had to move out of here? And you guys had cabinets falling off the hinges for at least a year."

"That we did. Drove me crazy."

"Well, you've done an amazing job fixing it up."

"I wanted a nice place for the boys to grow up, and we don't have a lot of money. I mean, we get by fine, but there's not a lot left over for extras, especially now that I'm home. I just had to learn to be more creative."

"I'm sure they love it. And look at these windows. I've never seen anything like them."

"Aren't they great?" Finn asked. Olivia laughed, the exchange an inside joke that Gracie was not privy to. Olivia turned to Gracie, rolling her eyes.

"Finn helped put them in. He and Grant didn't know what the heck they were doing with that first window." She pointed to the large window furthest away from where they were standing. "Anyway, he never lets me forget it, and he loves taking all the credit."

They heard a large bang and then Grant stuck his head through the slider. "Olivia, honey, I need another spatula. Judd got a hold of mine and dropped it and the plate I was using on the deck. Do you mind?" He smiled when he saw Gracie and Finn. "You guys hungry?" he asked, grinning.

"Famished," Gracie said. "You need some help corralling them?"

Grant looked up over his shoulder, eyeing his sons.

"Good luck with that," he said, opening the slider more so she could step through. "They're out of control." As soon as he said it, Ezra took a water gun and squirted Judd with it. The two boys ran around the yard in circles, shooting water up into the air in between trying to hit each other.

"Boys! Didn't I just tell you to wash up?" They both stopped, long enough for Olivia to turn her attention away, and then they were after each other again. Olivia handed the clean spatula to Grant and picked up the plate that had fallen, spraying hamburger grease across the deck boards. "Can I get you guys something to drink?"

"I'll take a beer," Finn said, watching Ezra and Judd.

"How 'bout you, Gracie?"

"A beer would be great."

Olivia returned to the kitchen. Grant looked up from the grill. He looked at Finn, but his eyes were hidden behind the sunglasses he wore. "You two been seeing the sights today?"

Finn chuckled, turning to face his friend. "You remember Gracie grew up with us, right? She's seen all the sights there are to see around Glenwood."

"Right. And Ashland?"

"Finn's going to show me around in a few days."

Grant flipped a few of the burgers over. "How long you in town for?"

"Just a week," she said, sitting down on a big deck chair with red cushions.

"And you head back to—Pomroy, isn't it?"

"That's right."

"You like it there?" he asked, looking up from the grill. "I took Olivia one weekend. We went to dinner, stayed at a really nice bed and breakfast. It wasn't long after Judd was born, you know, a parents-only weekend away."

"Yeah, it's nice. I mean, it's about the size of Ashland, but probably a bit nicer."

"I don't know, Gracie. I bet you'd be surprised with how different Ashland is today. It's a different city than it was when we were young."

"Really? I can't imagine it's changed that much," she said, interested.

Grant put the lid back down on the grill and sat down on the chair next to her. Finn watched them both from the opposite side of the deck.

"Well, I guess you'll see what I mean when Finn takes you over there. They've done a lot of work to it, adding parks, trying to attract people down there and get people invested in the city again."

"Makes sense," Gracie said.

Olivia emerged from the house once again, holding several bottles of beer. "There's plenty more in the house, so help yourselves when you need another."

"Thanks, Liv," Grant said, taking a bottle from her and handing it to Gracie before standing up and returning to his grill duties. Olivia handed a bottle to Finn, then sat down where Grant had been.

"I'm glad you guys could come tonight. You know we would have tried to go out, but the boys are so rowdy, we thought this would be best."

"It's no problem, Olivia," Gracie said, leaning back in her chair, then stretching her arms out above her head. "This is perfect." She looked out over the yard, where the boys played, her eyes resting on the flowers at the end of the drive. Blocked on the west side by the garage, the alternating purple and white hydrangeas had flourished, creating a wall of color so vibrant that it almost sparkled. Gracie couldn't peel her eyes away.

"We planted those two summers ago," Olivia said. She swept a hair out from the clutches of her lashes, tucking it neatly behind her ear.

"They're gorgeous!" She stood, leaning over the deck to inspect them.

"The aluminum level out here is pretty low," Grant said. "That's why they look so dang good—that purple color just thrives out here."

"I wouldn't have taken you two for gardeners."

"Just tried our luck, really." He shrugged as if that was all there was to it, but Gracie knew better. She looked at Olivia, who gave her a wink, confirming what Gracie suspected, that she was tenderly caring for those flowers during the day, helping them bloom.

Grant took the burgers off the grill, retreating back into the house with the platter. Olivia followed him in, and Gracie could hear the hum of dishes clanking as they prepared everything. Ezra galloped across the yard before planting himself next to Finn on the top step of the deck. "Dinner ready yet?" he asked.

"Just about," Finn said, putting an arm around his shoulders. They sat there like that until Olivia opened the door again, calling for Judd, who was lying on his back in the middle of the yard.

"The only time that boy lies down is when I want him to do somethin'," she said, ushering them all in. "Get your plates, boys," she said. Ezra did as he was told. Judd, on the other hand, grabbed some blueberries and popped them into his mouth. He was about to go for some more when Olivia's voice ran out behind him. "Judd Elijah Dornan, you didn't get manners like that from me."

Judd eyed Gracie and Finn, then grabbed a plate and piled on the blueberries.

Once everyone was seated, they ate quietly, enjoying the taste of the berries, burgers, pasta salad and, Gracie's favorite, Cajun mashed sweet potatoes.

When they were through, Finn raised an eyebrow at the boys, a smile slowly spreading across his face. "Good thing you boys ate so well because Gracie here brought apple pie for desert!"

"Really?" Judd asked, his eyes hopeful. "Gracie, did you bring a pie?"

"I did."

"And we can have some?" he asked, somewhat tentatively, looking from Gracie to Olivia.

Olivia nodded and he rubbed his hands together, licking his lips at the same time. "Oh boy, Ezra, apple pie!"

"Yeah, and don't even think about stealin' bites of mine." Ezra crossed his arms in front of him.

"There's enough for everyone to have their own piece," Gracie said.

"That don't matter to Judd!" Ezra said, scowling. "He sneaks bites when you're not lookin'!"

"Yeah, you might want to keep an eye on him," Grant said. "Especially since you're sitting next to him."

Gracie eyed the little boy on her left, but he just grinned.

"Ah, I bet Gracie doesn't mind sharing her dessert." Finn said, moving his plate over and leaning onto one arm. "Do you, Gracie?"

Judd stared up at her, waiting for her to respond. "I suppose I wouldn't mind if someone stole a small bite," she said.

"I don't take bites from the company," Judd said, sticking out his tongue at Ezra.

Ezra rolled his eyes, watching as Olivia cleared off the plates and began to cut into the pie. "Can I have a big piece, Mama?"

"Me too, me too!" Judd yelled, climbing off his chair and scampering into the kitchen, right on Olivia's heels.

"Alright, alright," Grant said, interrupting the pleading. "You get what your mama gives you. And Judd, get back over here and let her get things ready without worrying she might trip over you."

"But, Daaad!"

Grant shot a look at his son, who hurried back to his chair, hopping up onto his knees to watch Olivia carry plates to the table. Gracie could see every part of him wanted to lunge forward to grab the plate, but Grant was watching his every move, so he waited for Olivia to set it down in front of him. When she did, he gazed at it admiringly before scooping up a bite the size of Alaska and shoveling it into his mouth. His cheeks were so full that as he smiled at the taste of it, he had trouble chewing it up. Grant just shook his head.

"It's always interesting around here," Finn said, stealing a glance at Gracie.

Olivia plopped back down in her chair, taking a deep breath before biting into her piece. When she had swallowed up the first bite, she raised an eyebrow at Finn, her fork frozen in the air. "You don't even know the half of it," she said. Then she scooped up another bite, closing her eyes as the chaos continued to swirl around her.

Ezra adjusted the guitar on his knee and Finn leaned down over him. He strummed a few chords and looked up at Finn, expectantly. "What?" Finn asked. "You've got it. You've been playin' this song for a few weeks now."

"Yeah, but never in front of anyone."

"Aw, you're doing fine."

Ezra strummed some more before looking up at his audience of two. "Well?"

"Perfect," Gracie said. "Finn, you're a good teacher."

"Oh, I haven't done much to help him. He just watches me play and picks things up."

Ezra smiled at Finn's compliment.

"You and Tucker still play together?" Gracie asked.

"We do. Just a couple times a month over in Ashland with a few other guys I met at school." Finn leaned back in his chair. The fire was low in the pit, and Olivia was walking around in the brush, picking up sticks to feed it with. Gracie pulled on her jacket, a ratty old denim coat she'd had forever. It was nothing special, but it served its purpose. "You probably wouldn't even recognize Tuck now."

"Oh really?"

"He looks like a young Santa Claus," Ezra said, laughing as he set the guitar down and bounded up the yard.

Finn nodded, a smile breaking out over his face. "He's got a beard down to here." His hands went to his face in an effort to emphasize the bushiness of Tuck's beard. "He does some backup singing now, too."

"Now, that I don't believe." Tucker Rainey had barely even wanted to play with Finn back in high school. He'd been the classic introvert, using music to express himself, but never playing for a crowd. Their senior year, though, he'd lost a bet to Finn, having to overcome his fears and play with him at the talent show that year. It had nearly killed him. Finn almost let him out of it, but he'd said a bet is a bet and showed up at the show, sweating bullets.

"It's true."

Gracie shook her head in disbelief. "I'll have to come check it out sometime."

"You could, you know. We're playing next week."

"I need to head back after the funeral. I've got work."

"Yeah." Finn said as he got up from his chair. "The real world calls." He turned to Gracie. "Want another?" he asked, motioning to his empty beer bottle.

"Nah, I'm good." Gracie slouched down in her chair hugging her knees to her chest. The crackling fire made her feel ready to drift off to sleep, something she really didn't want to do. Grant and Olivia would be happy to let her stay, but with two young kids in the house, that'd mean an early wakeup call, too. She stood up from her chair, her eyes adjusting to the darkness as she scanned the yard for Olivia.

"Going somewhere?" Finn asked, returning from his jaunt to the house.

"Back to the hotel. I'm about to fall asleep right here by this pit." She yawned as if on cue. "Where's Olivia?"

"She's cleaning up in the kitchen. Grant's still putting the kids down." He cocked his head, looking at her. "Can I ask you something, Gracie?"

She rubbed at her eyes, yawning again. "Sure."

"I want you to be honest, because I've run over and over those last days in my head. And every time, we're laughing, talking like nothing's wrong. I can't figure it out, and I feel like maybe, if I knew, you know, what happened..."

"Finn, I..."

"No, Gracie," he said, not letting her finish. He knew when he was about to get shot down. "Hear me out. Please. I loved you. I thought you loved me. When you left..." His words floated off as if they hurt him too much say, but then he found them again and they came out fast and forceful. "At first I hated you. I was furious, angry at everyone and everything. It took a long time for that anger to go away, but now that you're here again..." He sighed. "When I saw you in the lobby, I felt relief, seeing you and knowing you were alright. Seeing it with my own eyes. But, now I'm growing angrier by the day." She could see it written all over his face. She needed to tell him, but she knew it would change everything. "I'm beside myself that you won't tell me what happened. That you decided our fate when you left. That I had no say in it."

Gracie could feel the tears in her eyes, and she tried to blink them back. "I was young, Finn. I made a lot of bad choices back then. I thought they were right at the time." She crossed her arms in front of her chest, rubbing her arms to comfort herself.

"Just tell me what happened." His face was tired, sad. It hurt her to know she was the cause of his pain.

"Why can't you just let it go?" She forced the words out, but the coldness of her question was easier to bear than facing the truth.

"Let it go?" he yelled across the flames at her. "What do you think I've been trying to do all these years?"

"I'm sorry," she whispered.

They both turned as they heard the back door to the house open. It was a welcome escape from their heated discussion. Gracie wiped her eyes. Finn cleared his throat.

"Hey, you guys. S'mores?" Olivia asked, holding up a package of marshmallows from the back steps.

"Sure," Gracie hollered back, not looking at Finn.

"You're not going?" Finn asked, his voice low.

Gracie didn't respond. She simply sat back down and waited for Olivia to join them.

She could feel Finn's eyes on her, but she refused to meet his gaze. As Olivia set up the s'mores fixin's, Grant emerged from the house with a few more bottles of beer. She knew their conversation wasn't over. Finn needed to know, and maybe she needed to tell him, so they both could move on, but now wasn't the time.

"So," Grant said as he took a seat by Gracie. "What'd I miss?"

Finn's voice sounded far away when he answered. "Absolutely nothing."

5.

WHILE EVERYONE IN TOWN SEEMED TO GOSSIP ABOUT HER daddy, the drunk, Finn never talked about it. When he came to the house, he spoke only to Hannah, and sometimes Mama, or nobody, finding his way to her room where they would shut the rest of the house out. Even as kids, he seemed to know that she wanted to escape. They rarely stayed there, taking off to trek through the wooded areas in the neighborhood, or finding their way to Olivia's house, where the homemade cookies and welcoming hugs from her own parents, gave her a sanctuary to retreat to.

That's why, when Finn came down the walk, hearing Jack Brannen's shouts from inside the house, he knew better than to wait for Gracie outside. Still just a boy, he hadn't put much thought into it at all. He'd known the right thing was to find Gracie and get her the hell out. But he hadn't anticipated how bad it had gotten. He hadn't realized how much Gracie was hurting until that night. So when he found out, he vowed he wouldn't let anyone hurt her again.

A bottle broke against the wall, the pieces falling like embers, glistening as they hit the floor, their sharp edges taunting Gracie, challenging her.

"Where you think you're goin'?" he yelled. For some reason he had chosen tonight to come after her, when usually he could care less what she did or who she did it with.

"Out," she said, shrinking against the wall.

"With who? It's nearly dark out."

"It won't be dark for another hour, Daddy. Finn and I are just goin' down to the pond to fish."

"So, you're runnin' 'round with boys, then?"

"It's just Finn, Daddy. You've known him forever. Their family used to live next door, remember?"

"I remember. I remember his daddy parkin' on our lawn is what I remember." One time, Gracie thought. Finn's family had a party and asked Mama if they could move a car over to the edge of their front yard, to make room for their guests. Daddy had gone crazy when he came home and saw the car there, interrupting the party and causing a scene.

"It's just a half-mile up the road," she said.

"You're not goin' anywhere. Sit your butt down and be part of this family instead of runnin' off like you're too good for it."

"Jack," Mama came into the living room, looking around. "Have you seen my keys? I've got to head to work."

"No, I ain't seen your keys, woman."

Mama noticed Gracie there, then saw the broken bottle on the floor. "What's goin' on here?"

Jack Brannen lit a cigarette, letting it dangle from his lips. "This one thinks she's goin' out with Finn Miller."

"Where you goin', Gracie?" Mama asked, moving towards her.

"Just fishin' up at the pond," she said.

"That's alright, isn't it, Jack?"

"Hell no, it's not alright. She don't need to be runnin' around with that boy."

Mama sucked in her breath, putting her hands on her hips as Daddy took a drag on his cigarette. "And why not?"

"Why not? Because that family looks down on us. You want to be friendly with people like that?" He spat the words at them, a mix of saliva and beer shooting from his mouth onto the carpet below him. No wonder it always smelled in here, Gracie thought.

"Jack, you're not thinkin' clear. She goes fishin' with Finn every..."

"I don't care if she goes fishin' with that boy every day. He's no good."

That was a laugh. Gracie was only nine years old, but she already knew Finn was way too good for the likes of her. Valerie Worley had said as much the last day of third grade. "Why's Finn hangin' out with Gracie Brannen?" she'd said. "Don't he know she's the daughter of scum? That's what my Ma says." Gracie had cried the whole way home, thinking it was just a matter of time before Finn came to his senses and left her for a more popular set of friends.

"Gracie, go on. It's fine." Mama started looking for her keys again.

"You deaf, woman? I just said no!"

"And I said yes. She's got to have friends, Jack. You can't keep her locked in here, scared to come out of her bedroom."

"I can do whatever the hell I want. I'm her daddy." He stood up, moving toward Mama with a fierceness in his eyes. His ability to appear totally sober surprised Gracie.

"And I'm her mama." She remained calm, standing her ground.

The thing about Mama was that she hated confrontation. She and Hannah were cut from the same cloth, striving above all else to keep the peace. Gracie's knack for doing the complete opposite was a quality she knew she got from her dad, but even though she hated the thought of being like him in any way, it was so ingrained in her that she couldn't run from it, couldn't help but lash out. But, for some reason, this time, Mama didn't back down. She stood, her arms crossed staring Daddy down, so Daddy did the only thing he could do. He reached out, his hands swift and strong, grabbing Gracie and pulling her to him, like a pawn in a chess game.

Gracie yelped, partly in fear, partly in surprise.

"She's not goin' anywhere."

"Let go of her, Jack," Mama pleaded, her hand reaching for Gracie.

But he held her tighter. The smell of alcohol overwhelming now that she was so close to him. She couldn't remember the last time her daddy had touched her in any way, and now he grabbed her so forcefully there were marks on her arm already where his fingers pushed against her skin.

Gracie knew Mama was going to be late to work. Her shift began at six every night, and it was almost that now.

"Mama, it's alright. Go on ahead to work." Gracie didn't recognize her own voice. It sounded more like a meek field mouse squeaking from underneath the cornstalks.

She didn't move, and neither did Daddy.

"Let go of her," Mama repeated.

His grip loosened on her arm, and he took another drink. Gracie, too afraid to move in any direction, stayed there next to him until she heard Mama's voice, beckoning her. "C'mon over here, Gracie."

She took a step towards Mama, who nodded, reassuring her. In the next second, she was on the ground. There was no way she would have seen it coming. He moved so quickly, and his fist hit her so forcefully, that she had no time to react, even if she had. The blow came from behind, knocking the wind out of her as she fell to the ground. She fell forward fast, on her wrists, and she heard Mama cry out as Gracie hit the floor hard. Daddy lunged at her again, and Mama grabbed at his arm, trying to pull him off. That's when she heard the door fly open.

"Get off her now!"

Gracie looked up, seeing Finn enter, his fishing pole in his hand. His face was contorted in anger and he was breathing hard, as if he'd been running. He was so small, but in that moment he looked older. She thought she might be afraid of him if it was anyone else.

Her daddy looked up in surprise, not sure what to do. Gracie took the moment to catch her breath before pulling herself to her feet.

"You ever do that again…" Finn stopped, knowing a nine-year-old boy didn't have much to threaten a grown man with. But it didn't matter. It was enough.

He grabbed Gracie's hand and pulled her through the front door. Daddy slumped back down on the couch.

Neither said a word as they ran the rest of the way to the pond. They were both sweating and out of breath by the time they got to it. When they came to a stop, Finn looked back in the direction they'd come. "When'd it get so bad, Gracie?" he asked, his voice angry.

She didn't respond. Had it ever been any other way?

"What am I s'pose to do now? Let you go back there?"

"Mama's there. Hannah's there. He'll sleep it off."

"How many times has he hit you like that?"

"He hasn't."

"Don't lie to me, Gracie."

"I'm not. I'd tell you if he had, Finn. That was the first time. It surprised me as much as you."

He was quiet a moment, then walked over to her, putting his fishing pole down. "Turn around."

"Why?"

"Let me see your back."

"Aw, I'm fine, Finn."

"For Christ's sake, Gracie. Turn around and let me see you're okay."

She frowned. "I just ran the whole way here. I'm fine."

Finn crossed his arms, waiting. She scowled, but turned, lifting her shirt so he could look at her back. She felt his fingers run down the center, as if he were gently tracing something. She winced and dropped her shirt again, turning around. Finn's face had twisted itself into a mix of horror and rage.

"If he puts his hands on you again, I swear I'll kill him."

She nodded, not knowing what to say.

Finn turned away and walked in front of her a few steps. She stood, frozen in place, her heart racing. She felt, in that moment, a need to comfort him. Finn stopped and turned to look at her. His cheeks were burning red and even in the darkness she could see the glistening of his eyes. "You're my best friend," he said.

"I know, Finn," she said.

He reached out, tucking a hair behind her ear. It felt strange, like something done in the movies Mama watched sometimes on TV, not real life. At least not hers.

"I'll be okay," she said, trying to reassure him. And then, to reassure herself, she added, "Everything will be okay."

Hannah pulled her hair back off her shoulders and secured it tightly with a hair tie. She'd gotten Gracie out of the house, and now she and Dave were moving chairs, stacking plates and preparing food before getting ready for Mama's funeral. It had been a blessing that Olivia had offered to take Cayla for the morning and bring her to the church later. And it gave Hannah time to reflect on everything, which she found she really needed after the whirlwind of events that had befallen their home in the past few weeks.

She started wiping down the kitchen counters with a damp rag, letting crumbs fall to the floor, knowing she'd vacuum them up soon enough. Her hands moved quickly, and she wondered if she were going too fast, leaving things not quite as clean as she wanted them.

That morning she had crawled out of bed and immediately started to move about the house. When Gracie emerged from Cayla's room she'd looked around her, wanting to help, but Hannah wanted her out. She needed some time to herself before the chaos ensued, before she had to put on her older sister hat, before she had to stand in a line thanking people for their sympathies. Yes, before she could be strong for everyone else, she needed time to be weak. She thought, at least on this day, she was allowed that right.

Dave was setting up chairs in the backyard, and the kitchen now sparkled. Everything was ready, except her.

Walking to the bathroom, she turned on the faucet and splashed some water on her face. Her eyes looked sunken and there were dark circles beneath them. She'd looked the same for over a week. Sickly. The way Mama had looked near the end. She needed to spruce herself up. Pulling the shower curtain back, she turned on the water and waited for it to heat up, letting the steam fill the bathroom. Quickly, she undressed and stepped under the water, immediately feeling relaxed. She closed her eyes, the feel of the water hitting her face calming her, allowing her to slip into a meditation of sorts.

When she and Gracie were kids, Mama had prepared them together for events like this, giving them a bath, dressing them, sometimes in matching outfits, curling their hair and, when they were older, spritzing them with a tiny bit of her perfume, all the while letting them joke and giggle with each other, oblivious to whatever occasion had called for this special activity bringing them together and relishing in it.

Hannah, being the daughter bearing most of Mama's qualities, had always felt close to her and later, when she was older, responsible for her. She knew Gracie felt outside of this connection they shared, and no matter how much Hannah tried to include her, somehow there was always distance between the two of them and her younger sister. When Gracie disappeared, leaving them both behind, Mama had been quick to come to her defense, while Hannah had been annoyed and resentful.

"She's got her reasons, Hannah," Mama had said to her one night, not long after Gracie had gone.

"I don't understand it. She was going to leave anyway. Why do it this way? She didn't even tell Finn where she was going. She didn't even tell him she *was* going!"

Mama's shoulders had slumped forward. "You know our Gracie. She's not one to be tied down. Maybe she just needs time to figure things out on her own."

"She's being selfish, Mama. She's only thinking about herself."

"She's got her own life to live. Maybe the only way she knows how to do that is by setting out on her own. Completely. Maybe this is just how she has to do it."

"Stop making excuses for her, Mama! She's left us without a word. Aren't you upset at all?"

"Of course I'm upset," she'd said. "But, Hannah, she's my daughter. She's your sister. We have to support what she needs out of this life, what she wants."

The two women had stared at each other, Hannah from where she stood in the living room and Mama from the kitchen table, both with pain in their eyes.

"She'll come back," Mama had whispered, finally, letting the words fall from her tongue like coins in a wishing well, full of hope and dreams and determination.

"It's Gracie. She'll never come back. Not after leaving this way. She's too damn stubborn like Daddy was."

"She'll come back," Mama repeated. Then, looking up at Hannah, she'd narrowed her eyes at her oldest daughter. "And you'll welcome her home, Hannah. You'll forgive her for this."

All Hannah could do was nod. And she'd done it, welcomed her back without a harsh word. But it had been hard, harder than she had thought it would be.

The water began to turn cold, so she switched it off and reached for her towel hanging on the back of the door. The bathroom had filled up with steam, fogging up the mirror, and when she opened the door, her lungs took in the coolness of the new air seeping into the room. She walked to her bedroom, throwing the towel on the bed and slipping into her underwear and an old lace bra. She hadn't had time to shop for anything new. When Mama had entered hospice care, she'd been there every day, leaving everything else at home to Dave to worry about, including Cayla. It had been a hard few weeks, saying goodbye, watching Mama slowly slip away. But she had been there at the end, watched Mama take her last breath, holding her hand as she went.

She pulled on her dress, doing her best to zip it up, but unable to pull it all the way to the top. Dave could help, she thought, but instead of yelling for him, she simply sat down on the bed, her wet hair falling down, still sending drips of water down her neck.

Mama hadn't wanted her to be angry with Gracie, but now that she was finally alone, she had time to really think about what she felt, and she was angry.

Family was supposed to be there for each other. Where had her sister been all this time?

She took a deep breath and got up, walking back to the bathroom and pulling out the hair dryer.

Once this day was behind them and the funeral over, she would demand to know. Gracie might be able to disappear for ten years, but now that she was back, she was going to answer for it. She owed it to Mama, and if Hannah was being completely honest, her sister owed it to her, too.

6.

THE SMELL OF BREAD FILLED HER UP AS SHE WALKED INTO the bakery. Hannah had mentioned the place, a random tidbit about Saturday morning tradition, meeting Mama for a croissant, a bagel or whatever was pleasing to the eye, and stomach, that day. Today, Gracie saw raspberry and apricot scones, blueberry muffins with streusel topping, cherry and pineapple Danish rolls, long johns and good old-fashioned cake donuts.

Gracie was eyeing the case at the front of the small shop when she heard the voices behind her, two customers sitting at a small table in the corner.

"Luke's got a scholarship to MSU, all four years, playin' baseball," a woman with white hair down to her shoulders said as she nudged her glasses up on her nose.

"You must be so proud," her companion, a woman who must have been a few years younger, replied. Her short hair looked messy, going in every direction, but had been styled that way. They were the only other two customers in the bakery, sharing the latest gossip Gracie guessed, and plotting their way to the top of Glenwood's social ladder.

"It's hard for these kids to get outta this town," she said. "They all want to, but only the hardest working ones make it out."

Gracie kept her attention on the baked goods in front of her, trying not to listen in.

"Can I help you, Miss?" a teenage boy asked from behind the counter. He stopped walking to the back room and stood, waiting.

"Yes, thank you," she said. She pointed to the raspberry scone. "I'll take one of those and a white mocha."

"What size?"

"The largest you've got," she said, considering how exhausted her body felt. The emotional toll Mama's death had taken, along with running around with Cayla, the anxious feelings she got whenever she was around Finn. She felt like she needed a vacation.

The younger woman at the table held up a brochure. "Have you seen these new condos going up off of 18th Street?" she asked.

Her friend shook her head. "You plannin' on movin'?"

"Thinkin' about it. Rich is getting close to retirement. Maybe we'll start an adventure, go someplace new." Gracie knew that was unlikely. Once your roots were planted in Glenwood, they usually stayed there, so deep in the soil that no matter how much you wanted to leave there was no way you could.

"Well, you know who you need to talk to, then, is that Finn Miller. He's quite the realtor I hear. Grew up here, too, you know."

"Miller..." the spiky-haired woman said, trying to place the name. "His daddy was Troy Miller? Worked for the city?"

"That's the one."

"That man was eye candy for sure," she said. "His son the same?"

"Oh yes, still available, too, from what I hear."

"I'll have to tell Georgia to look him up."

The white-haired woman looked surprised. "She and Wyatt broke up? Rita! Why didn't you say something?"

Shaking her head, Rita frowned. "Oh, you know I was plannin' the engagement party already! Now, I've got to tell everyone it's off. It makes me look ridiculous."

"That'll be five-seventy." The boy behind the counter smiled politely, placing her scone and drink on the counter. Gracie dug in her purse, taking out a ten.

"Keep the change," she said, reaching for her purchase.

"Thanks!" he said, surprised.

It was the least she could do if he had to continue listening to the inane conversation beside her. She took a sip from the cup. Even in the middle of summer she enjoyed a good gourmet coffee. She'd tried the iced versions, but they'd never had the same appeal.

Walking from the bakery, she wondered if she should call Finn and let him know he was the hot topic among Glenwood's social climbers, but, if the other night had showed her anything, he was probably already well aware.

She walked around to her car and opened the door, steadying her scone atop her coffee as she slid into the seat.

The funeral would start in a few hours' time. Hannah and Dave were readying their home for visitors after. Olivia had offered to take Cayla for a few hours to play with the boys so they had time to set things up. Gracie had offered to help, but ultimately felt in the way as Hannah and Dave moved around the house, dancing a routine that they'd clearly done many times before, barely speaking to each other as they glided past each other, setting out dishes and wiping off counters. When Hannah suggested Gracie take some time for herself, suggesting Lyn's Bakery, too, Gracie had reluctantly made her way out of the house.

She chomped down on the scone. Scones had always tasted a little dry to Gracie, but this one was buttery and flaky, leaving her completely satisfied with the purchase. To her surprise there was a hint of almond, too, and she wondered if all the other scones she had ever tried had been made wrong.

Taking another bite, she set the rest of the scone down on the napkin in her passenger seat and started up the car, not sure where she was headed next. She supposed she could always head to Grant and Olivia's, but knew

Olivia would soon be getting them all ready for the funeral. She thought of the black floral dress she'd brought that was now hanging on the back of the door in Cayla's room. It wouldn't take her long to get ready. She'd just need a few minutes to curl her hair and apply some makeup. She rarely wore makeup anyway, and thought it ironic that she'd be putting it on before a funeral, knowing there would be tears that would leave it streaking down her face.

She drove around the town square and made her way to the old neighborhood. As she turned onto the street, she slowed down in front of the old house. It looked the same, but the street did not. Where open fields had been, there were some new homes. A daycare had gone in almost directly behind the house, making the property look smaller than she remembered, or maybe that's just how memory worked. Things always seem big until you stand back a bit. The paint was chipping in several places she could see from the street, meaning up close it was probably even more obvious. Weeds had grown in where Mama's garden had been and an old garden gnome had tipped over beside it, forgotten in the overgrown brush. She pulled off to the side of the road just as her phone rang. Holding it up, the name Stella appeared on the screen and she couldn't help but smile.

"Hello?" she answered.

"Gracie! I didn't think I'd catch you. Isn't the funeral today?" Stella's voice was a comfort right now, her nurturing voice radiating affection and light. In all the time Gracie had known her, Stella had been the substitute mother she'd needed, never replacing her own, but guiding her and lending support when needed.

"Yes, a bit later. How are you?"

"I'm good. I'm good. But I don't want to talk about me. How is it being back?"

"It's going surprisingly well," she said, looking around. "I have a lot to tell you, but I'm...well, I guess I don't have a lot of time right now. Stella, it is *so* good to hear your voice."

"Oh, and it's good to hear yours. I've been thinking about you every minute, Gracie. Well, every free minute, anyway. I just wanted to tell you that. Today will be hard and you need to know someone's rooting for you."

Gracie looked back across the street, thoughtful. "You always know just what to say. And your timing couldn't be better. Thank you."

"Alright, well, I've got to get going. Call me if you need anything."

"I will. Bye, Stella."

Gracie put the phone down and got out, her mind swirling with memories that had been pushed away, but now broke free as she stared out at the familiar neighborhood. She could see the old treehouse out back. Her daddy had built it when Hannah was about a year old, right before they'd found out Mama was pregnant with Gracie.

From the looks of it, the house was empty. Maybe it had been that way since Mama moved out. A few of the houses on this block looked deserted. She wondered if Finn's place, a few blocks to the north, was in the same shape, or if his parents still lived there, caring for it as they had so many years ago.

Gracie took a sip of her coffee and walked to the front door. She opened the screen and knocked.

"You lookin' for someone?"

Gracie turned to see a man across the street. He had a scruffy beard, and he stood as she imagined a bear would if it had been as skinny as this man.

"Does anyone live here?" she asked, shielding her eyes with the same hand holding her cup.

"Nah, nobody's lived there for quite some time." He raised a bushy eyebrow at her. "Lookin' to buy?"

"Oh no," she said. "I actually used to live here."

His eyes narrowed. "Gracie?" he asked.

Startled, she moved back down the walk, leaning forward. "Yes..."

"Van Rundee!" he said, patting his chest. "You remember me?"

Van Rundee. She remembered him alright. "I barely recognized you!"

"Well, I reckon I look a bit different than you remember." Gracie approached him tentatively, wanting to hug him.

"You do indeed." She looked to the house behind him. "Didn't your parents live a few houses that way?" She pointed to the left.

"Still do. I bought this one so I could help 'em look after things. They're gettin' older, you know. Need a young, strappin' lad to help around the house."

The Rundees had been in their mid-forties when Van had come along. They'd tried for years to get pregnant, according to Mama. By 40, Mrs. Rundee had accepted she would never have children, and a few years later, she was pushing Van out on her kitchen floor. He'd come so fast they hadn't had time to get to the car, let alone drive to the hospital. Mama had helped catch Van, too, if she remembered correctly. Both she and Hannah had served as babysitters over the years. He must've been about ten or eleven when she left.

"How are they doing?"

"Aw, they're gettin' on well enough." Gracie wondered if Van ever felt cheated, having parents so much older. He didn't seem too affected. "Heard about your own mama. Sorry to hear it."

"Thank you," she said.

He shuffled his feet in the dirt. "Now, I know I haven't seen you around these parts in a long while. Where you livin' now?"

"Pomroy," she answered, taking another sip. "Hannah lives on the other side of town. She's married. Has a daughter, Cayla."

"Yeah, I know. Seen 'em at church a few times if I recall. She's always pleasant to me."

Van scratched his head and squinted his eyes. "It's open," he said, nodding toward the house. "I mean, if you want to take a look."

Gracie tried to reconcile the young man in front of her with the boy she used to chase down the street, not wanting to come in for the night and take a bath. She'd yelled Van Rundee's name at the top of her lungs more times than she could remember, and carried him over her shoulder as he squealed and kicked his feet in her face. Now here he stood, grown-up and hospitable.

"I might just do that," she said.

"Well, alright. Good to see you, Gracie." He casually saluted her then turned back to his house.

Before Gracie turned the knob on the front door, she turned back and saw him starting up the mower. A breeze blew through, making her arm hair stand on end, and she felt a sense of déjà vu. No matter, she thought, and pushed open the door to her childhood home.

As she walked into the house, it wasn't the dampness she noticed. The windows were open and she smelled the mildew wafting up from the thick carpet. In the darkness, the place looked alright, but where the light shone in from outside, she could see where the walls crumbled and spider webs hung from the ceiling. No, when she walked through the door, it was the dinginess of it. Had it looked that way when she'd lived here, too?

Closing the door behind her, she made her way to the middle of the house, standing adjacent to the hallway that led to all of the bedrooms. It was much smaller than she remembered, back before she'd been out in the world, when all she'd had were dreams of a different future from the one she saw all around her.

The place had been emptied of furniture, which one would have thought would make it seem bigger, and it made Gracie sad. She'd grown up here. Her first steps had been in this house, her first words. All the events that wove together a childhood. Her childhood.

She turned and made her way down the hallway, opening the doors as she went. Mama's room was the biggest but had the smallest window. A plastic bag lay on the floor where her bed had once been, the only item in the room. She walked in and picked it up, balling it up in her fist, the plastic crinkling as her fingers tightened around it. She sat down, remembering the times she had come into the room to find Mama crying because they were late on a bill, or when Daddy was still around, trying to shake off whatever awful comments he'd made to her that day. Gracie would crawl up beside her as she wiped away her tears, unsuccessfully trying to hide her sadness. She'd clamp her arms around her younger daughter, needing a relief from the pain of the world, and Gracie tried to give it to her, all the while wishing for a time when it was no longer her burden.

Her feelings about Mama, she'd discovered, varied from memory to memory. She found herself wishing for her Mama's smile, her laugh, which had changed after Daddy left from a tentative chuckle under her breath to a big belly laugh she didn't try to control. Other times, she pictured her mother in those vulnerable times when her daddy had still been around, and she shuddered. Her feelings confused her, and she wondered if all children felt such conflicting feelings towards their parents. She knew there were, what one would call, "normal" families out there. Finn's had been that way, and Olivia's. Grant's had been a little rougher around the edges, but not nearly as chaotic as Gracie's.

The room still smelled of Mama's perfume somehow, or Gracie knew now, the cheapest bottle from the town's only department store. She breathed it in, wishing she could smell it on Mama's skin.

Reluctantly, she moved down the hallway, past Hannah's room and a tiny bathroom to the end of the hall, where her room sat, the door open and inviting.

It was the same color of sky blue, the color she had painted it when she was ten years old, not wanting the bubblegum pink color it had been since a few months before Mama and Daddy had brought her home from the hospital. Mama had told her of the nights she'd spent painting it and how it had taken her more than a month to complete the project between her work shifts and caring for Hannah. Now there were more cracks in the walls, rippling down from the ceiling, than she remembered. A layer of dust sat on the windowsill where she'd sit, waiting to see Finn traipsing across the field behind her house.

Moving to the closet, she opened it, her eyes falling on a box at the top, sitting on a shelf, shoved way to the back, almost hidden from sight. But she had known it would be there. She reached up, straining her arms forward, grasping it between her fingers.

The lid was also covered in a thick layer of dust. She tried not to touch it while she lifted the lid slowly, setting it down on the floor beside her where she crouched over the box's contents.

Inside she found the switchblade. She picked it up, feeling it in her fingers, and she could almost feel Finn there. It was funny how certain things took you to another place, another time. She longed for that time, when their dreams were still possible, their hearts so sure. She set the blade down next to her, picking up the next item in the box. It was a photograph, faded with time. The one photo she had of all of them—Hannah, Mama and Daddy. They were standing in front of their church. Mama was holding a picnic basket and Daddy wore a big smile. Gracie had been young, a toddler at the time. She and Hannah wore matching dresses with yellow flowers dancing across the fabric, matching Mama's canary-colored cardigan sweater. They looked happy. Whether or not they actually had been that day was a mystery, Gracie being too young to remember. When she'd found the photo, hidden away in a stack of old magazines, she'd snatched it up, looking at it whenever she found herself wishing for something different, something other than empty beer cans and drunken arguments.

At the bottom of the box, she saw her graduation tassel, a friendship bracelet Hannah had made her and a program from their senior talent show. Beneath those items, she found the last item she had put in the box. Bagged up, covered in tissue, was the pregnancy test. She pulled it out, remembering her heart plummeting as she saw the results. It felt like yesterday, holding the bag in her hands. How could it have been ten years ago? She set it down, looking away, not able to reconcile her feelings. Then she noticed something else in the box. It had been hidden under the baggie, lying flat on the bottom so Gracie almost missed it. She pulled it out and flipped it over, recognizing the handwriting immediately. "Mama," she whispered to no one but herself. She read the words, then closed her eyes, letting the tears stream down her face, unable to stop them from falling.

Finally, she picked up the other items and put them back in the box, nestling it in the crook of her arm. She shut the door to her room and walked back out of the house, leaving the stale aroma behind her.

Van waved at her as she walked to her car. She waved back, albeit unenthusiastically.

She set the box in the passenger seat, staring at it a moment before starting up the car and making her way back to the motel, thinking of Mama's words.

I think of you often, Gracie, remembering your vitality, your love of life. I found this box by mistake as I cleaned out the house, knowing I have only so much time left. If you are reading this, then you came home, and I wish I could be there to see you, to hold my baby girl in my arms, as I've thought of doing every day since you left. Wrap your arms around that baby of yours, and never let go. I never will. I love you.

Oh, Mama, she thought. I love you, too.

The church was packed. With five minutes left until the service, there were only a few more spots left at the back. Gracie hadn't realized just how many people her mom had known. She recognized a lot of them. Sam, Nina and a few others from her mother's job at the bank were there.

She'd worked Saturdays there for a few years after Gracie's dad had left. Trudy, Evelyn and Frank had come together from her days working at the accounting office, where she'd worked as a secretary for many years. Family members Gracie hadn't seen in years were scattered throughout the pews. But there were many faces she didn't recognize. Hannah had leaned over and whispered names in her ear when they'd entered the church, Gracie and Hannah extending their hands out moments later to accept their sympathies.

"That's Marvin Yates. He went out with Mama a few times," she said as a thin man with graying hair took off his hat and looked toward them from the door. "They never hit it off, but he came by the house to check in on her from time to time."

And later, "That's Hal and Misty Swalert. They went to Mama's church, invited her to dinner sometimes when she wasn't coming over to see Cayla." Then a younger man with a moustache that reminded Gracie of an old western cowboy walked in, though he couldn't have been much older than Gracie.

"Who's he?" Gracie whispered, wondering what kind of connection her mother could have had with such an obvious outsider.

"That's Nick Tooley."

"Do we know him?"

"He and Mama became close these last few years." Hannah replied, looking in Nick's direction. "I met him a few times. He was nice, if a bit odd."

"He seems young. They weren't dating, were they?" Gracie asked, perplexed.

"I don't know." Hannah shrugged. "They always acted very secretive when they were together."

Nick Tooley looked over at them before taking a few paces and finding a seat at the back of the church, not joining the receiving line. "Something seems off about him," she said, not able to take her eyes from the man. "How old is he?"

"Gracie." Hannah sighed, letting her know the conversation was over. Gracie turned back to the line, but the man in the back of the church held her attention. He was young. In her opinion, much too young to be her mother's lover, if that was in fact even his relationship with her. Every so often he looked over his shoulder and met her gaze, causing her to jerk her head back abruptly. Something about him was familiar, but she couldn't place him.

"I'm so sorry, Gracie." Olivia came up behind her, grabbing her hands as she turned as Olivia was prone to do. "Just look at all these people. It's really something."

"It is," Gracie said. She took the opportunity to break from the receiving line and she pushed through a few people with Olivia at her heels, leading her to a corner of the room.

"Are you doing alright?" Olivia asked, her eyes wide with worry.

"So far, so good." She was, wasn't she? Or had she had time to even think about what this day meant?

"I'm glad. I've been worried about you."

"Me?" Gracie asked. "What for?"

"Well, for one, you didn't get to say goodbye. I mean, your mom didn't even tell you she was sick." That was true enough. She'd heard from her mother over the years but never anything about the tumor. "And for another, well," she hesitated, not wanting to say what was on her mind.

"Spit it out, Olivia."

"Well, you weren't here. You must feel so much guilt. I mean, I'm not saying you're guilty of something..." Olivia looked like she'd just shot herself in the foot.

Gracie held up her hand. "You're right. I am guilty of not being here. That was a choice I made. There were emails every so often. Not many, but some. It was easy for me to let the space fill up between us. I rarely checked in with her, even though I thought of her often. But she checked in on me from time to time.

Olivia looked surprised at this revelation. "You were in contact?"

"Some."

"I just thought..." Olivia's sentence faded off.

"I better get back," Gracie said, noticing her sister waving her back to the line. "We'll talk later, okay?"

Olivia nodded, then headed back to her seat.

The funeral was nice, as nice as a funeral could be, Gracie supposed. Her sister spoke in a touching eulogy that had people both laughing and crying. It was, no surprise to Gracie, perfect. It wasn't until Gracie began watching Cayla toward the end of the ceremony that she started to become emotional. Her mother had died, and she hadn't cried at the news. When she'd seen her mother's body, she hadn't cried. Yet in those final moments of the service, as she watched her young niece's tears fall, innocent trails of a grandchild's love, she hung her head and let her own tears roll down her cheek. Hannah put an arm around her shoulder, pulling her close as the organ played. She rested her head on her big sister's shoulder and closed her eyes, listening to the last notes, heavy in her ears. The sound took her back to Sunday mornings sitting in the too-big pew, her legs swinging back and forth beneath her. She spent the entire hour-long worship service wishing she could be crawling in the creek, catching frogs with Finn, or climbing up the treehouse, howling with laughter as they spied on their neighbors from their high-above fortress. Back when her father was still around, they'd never missed a Sunday at church. It seemed a bit hypocritical now. Their father, putting on a show for his acquaintances—her father didn't have any real friends—then coming home to get wasted, passing out before lunch and waking just in time to have it out with their mother for one reason or another, or more times than not, for no reason at all. He had a bad habit of blaming her for all his shortcomings. At first, their mother would shuttle them out the door, sending them to play in the yard, away from the tirade in the house. Eventually, Hannah took on the job of making them disappear before he even started in.

When the service ended, they rose from the pew and made their way to the car waiting outside that would take them to the cemetery. She and Hannah sat next to each other, their fingers intertwined. The ride was quiet but for the soft humming coming from Cayla as they turned onto the bumpy road that wandered through the gravesites. Gracie held onto Hannah as they walked to their mother's plot, as they watched her being lowered into the ground, and even as everyone dispersed, the two sisters stood, together, unable to let go. Dave departed with Cayla, who, between tears, had dashed off to chase a pair of squirrels running amongst the trees, the innocence of childhood finding her again. Gracie dabbed at her eyes with a tissue. "It was lovely, H."

Her sister turned, putting her arm around her. "It was," she said, studying Gracie. "Are you alright?"

Gracie nodded, though she felt light-headed. "Hannah..." Her sister's head snapped up at Gracie's use of her full name.

"What is it?" she asked.

"I have to tell you something," Gracie said. She looked down at the casket and let out a deep breath. This would take all her remaining strength. She felt guilty, knowing what she said next would place another weight on her sister's heart.

"When I left Glenwood, I was pregnant." The words fell out easily, considering how long she had been holding them in.

Hannah's body tensed and she sat up, alert. "What? What do you mean you were pregnant?"

Gracie closed her eyes, remembering. "I was pregnant," she said again. "I left because I was scared, and because a baby would've ruined all of Finn's plans."

Hannah shook her head in disbelief. "Did he say that?"

"He didn't know."

Gracie waited while Hannah took in this new information.

"Where is the baby?" Hannah whispered.

Gracie moved away, walking around the burial site, past the other headstones nearby to sit at a stone bench a few feet away. Her heart was pounding.

"Rosie didn't make it," she said, turning back to look at Hannah, who came to sit next to her. "She was stillborn."

Tears began to form in Hannah's eyes and she pulled Gracie into a tight embrace. Hugging Hannah was like hugging their mother. She enveloped Gracie wholly, tucking her head under her chin and stroking her cheek. Gracie held on, not wanting to let go. Her senses had gone into overdrive with the revelation, and she felt too exposed, too vulnerable.

After a moment, it was Hannah who pulled back. "Why didn't you tell me? Did Mama know?"

"Mama knew I was pregnant, but it was much later that she found out, around the time she started cleaning out the old house. But I didn't know that until this morning. She never knew anything about Rosie or what happened."

Hannah shook her head in disbelief. "I can't believe it."

"I wanted to tell her. And you. I think I thought I would. But then she came out, and she wasn't breathing..."

"Gracie..."

"I held her for hours, H. She was so beautiful." Gracie reached up and unclasped the necklace hanging around her neck. She opened it carefully, her daughter's small features staring back at her from inside the locket. She passed it to Hannah. "I couldn't tell anyone after that. I was so lost. I tried to go on with my life, but for a long time I was a mess. By the time I had found peace with it, I felt like it had been too long."

"Too long?" Hannah asked, not taking her eyes off of Rosie's picture.

"That I'd been away. I thought maybe it was too late to come back."

A tear fell down Hannah's face, but she didn't wipe it away. "I wish I'd known," she said. "I wish I could've been there for you."

"When you wrote me about Cayla, I just couldn't bear to come back. I wanted to, H. Oh, I did. But I was so hurt, I hadn't healed yet. It's a terrible reason, but it's the truth."

"I was so angry with you, too," Hannah said. "I begged Mama to tell me where you were. I thought she knew. I remember the first time you emailed us after you left you said you wanted us to know you were okay. We were so glad to hear from you. We thought it meant you might come home, but you never did. I wanted to give you a piece of my mind for sure." She shook her head, remembering.

"I was never sure what I wanted. In a lot of ways I felt like I couldn't come back..."

"I'm so sorry, Gracie." She handed the locket back. "You must have felt so alone."

Gracie didn't say anything. It was exactly what she'd felt for years, though it was no one's fault but her own. In trying to protect Finn from being tied down before he was ready, she'd run. In order to protect her family from the unbearable loss of her baby, she'd stayed away. In trying to protect herself, she'd cut off everyone from her old life and not turned back, wreaking havoc on the hearts of those she loved. All in a futile attempt to protect them. In the eyes of an eighteen-year-old, it had made sense. Now, it seemed unforgivable.

"Thank you," she said, finally.

"For what?"

"For not judging me."

"Gracie, we just lost our mother. I just found out you lost your daughter. The last thing I would think to do is judge you." Her voice was pained, and Gracie thought she looked a bit like a seasick cruise passenger. "C'mon, let's get out of here."

Gracie nodded and took her sister's hand, squeezing it tight as if she might bond them together, indefinitely.

7.

BACK AT HANNAH'S, THE WOMEN GATHERED IN THE LIVING room, making small talk in hushed voices. The men moved through the house, eager to make their way to the backyard to escape the sadness inside. They loosened their ties and sipped their beer as they made their way down the rickety steps leading to the patio, keeping an eye on the young ones happy to have a chance to play despite the circumstances.

Hannah was in the kitchen, putting another bowl of pasta salad together to set out on the kitchen table with the rest of the food they had prepared. Her tear-stained face showed the toll today had taken on her, but she worked meticulously, sashaying around the kitchen with ease as she whipped up the salad and gathered more ice for the coolers out back, keeping beers chilled for their friends and family.

"Such a shame," Gracie heard behind her. She turned to see her Aunt Helen reaching out for her. Mama's sister was a good fifteen years older. Mama had been a surprise to her parents, who, at the time, had almost been empty nesters. Uncle Billy had left town after high school, finding work a few towns over at the tire factory, while their Uncle Ollie had gone off to the community college. Helen had been their baby-until Mama came along.

"Aunt Helen," Gracie said. "It's so nice to see you. I'm so glad you could make it. Uncle Randy here?"

Helen's second husband, Randy, had been the only husband Gracie had known, being born after the first ran off with a younger version of Helen a few years before. Her mama had always said it was the ultimate mid-life crisis, and that he spent a good amount of their savings on a brand new top of the line fishing boat right before he and his new flame had skipped town, leaving poor Helen with the thing when she'd never before even cast a line. Mama said every time a creditor called Aunt Helen ran outside and spit on that blasted fishing boat. One time she'd gotten so mad, she grabbed fistfuls of dirt from the flower beds near her house and hurled them at the boat, cursing herself later when she had a potential buyer wanting to look at it and she had to get down on her hands and knees and vacuum up the dirt that had landed in the deck.

"Has a big case goin' on right now. Had to get back to it right after the funeral. We drove separately."

Randy was a district attorney a few counties over. He'd made a name for himself during one of the most sensational criminal trials the state had seen, when two men had brutally attacked a family after they'd returned home early from a vacation and found the men burglarizing their home. Randy was a quiet man, but Gracie had seen him in court once and had been amazed by his ruthlessness. It had been no surprise to her when they convicted the two men. You couldn't help but agree with Uncle Randy when you heard him speak. Being a man of few words, he chose them carefully, and it made him the perfect DA.

The man had to be in his mid-70s. "He's still working?"

"Oh, here and there when they need an especially sophisticated orator to get the job done."

Gracie smiled. She liked the thought of Uncle Randy putting the bad guys away even at his age. It made her feel like there were parts of this life you could count on to always be there. Uncle Randy, fighting the good fight, would always be there, and that was reassuring.

"You look beautiful, Gracie," her aunt said. She was a little woman. The fine lines had deepened across her face, but her skin was soft and supple, making her look younger than her years. She hunched forward, but moved quickly in spite of her ailment, whatever it was.

"Thank you."

"How long has it been since you've been back here?"

Gracie looked away, ashamed. "Ten years about."

"I thought so. You know, no matter how hard you try you can't stay away from your family forever. Somehow they always reel you back in."

She hadn't wanted that, had she? It sounded so cold, so heartless. But maybe she was those things.

"I left home as soon as I could," her aunt continued. "My parents were busy with your mom anyway by then. Sarah was hitting the terrible threes—it is the terrible threes, you know. Two is a breeze compared to three." Gracie nodded her head even though she had no experience with such things. "I stayed away almost a year until they reeled me back. I'd even been offered a job over in Sweetwater. Once I came back, though, I was done for. Married a year later, divorced two years later, married again. Worked out for the best though." Her aunt's words reminded her of Hannah telling her she wouldn't be going back to college. Everyone knew when you came back, you weren't leaving again. The thought was slightly unnerving considering she had also come back. But was it for good?

Aunt Helen hugged her then. Gracie had no idea what to say.

It didn't matter. Her aunt spotted Cayla at the back of the house, holding the door open with her foot and peeking out, yelling for Dave, and abruptly went after her, leaving Gracie standing awkwardly, watching her go.

Seeing her chance to escape, she quickly moved for the front door. The unoccupied porch swing slowly rocked back and forth, and Gracie walked over to it, sitting down sideways and pulling her knees up under her chin. She wrapped her arms around her legs, holding her dress to her to stay covered. After a while, she rested her head on her knees, watching the few people who hadn't made it into the house make conversation. At one point she saw

Cayla and Ezra dash across the yard, barefoot, hollering at the top of their lungs until Olivia came around from the back of the house and sat them down under one of the big shade trees and, Gracie assumed, explained the etiquette of a party that honored the deceased. Looking solemn, the three of them had then stood up and walked to the backyard again. It had made Gracie wish for her youth, a time when grief and sadness were fleeting, as a child's emotions could be.

Out of the corner of her eye, she saw Finn come up the lawn. He reached out for the door, not seeing her. She moved her body upright. "Hey, you," she said, startling him.

He let go of the door, seeing her for the first time. "What are you doing out here?" he asked, walking to her and taking a seat beside her on the swing.

"Thinking."

He nudged her shoulder. "You sure that's such a good thing?"

She laughed, liking the way sitting next to him felt. Liking the way he smelled, like expensive aftershave and oranges. "You don't like your women thinking too much?" she chided.

"My women, huh?"

She shrugged. Why had she said that, anyway?

He tapped her forehead. "What's going on in there?"

Too many thoughts floated around her head. She couldn't decide what to focus on. Her mind was like a spinning top, the painted images meshed together as one blurry image.

"I wish I had seen her one more time," she said, finally.

Finn nodded. He seemed relaxed, more so than she had seen him any other time since she'd been back. He put his hand on hers. "I'm sure if she has any say about it now, she's seeing you."

Gracie looked up at Finn, then looked past him to the sky, wanting with all her being to believe that was true.

"I'm not sure," she said. "If she's looking down here she could be cursing my name, thinking up ways to get back at me for abandoning her."

"I don't think your mama could curse anyone's name. She lived with your daddy how many years? Never once did I hear her say a bad word about the man."

"That's true," Gracie said. She kept forgetting how Finn's life intertwined with hers. How their pasts collided, almost every memory a shared experience.

"She loved you," he said.

Gracie leaned into him, needing his words to assuage the guilt she felt.

"I used to complain about her all the time, Finn. Do you remember?" Her voice was soft, afraid to admit such truths. "I thought she was spineless. I felt sorry for her. I never wanted to be like her. Even after Daddy left, and she didn't have to take his shit anymore, I didn't respect her like I should have. And I hated the thought of being like her. What kind of daughter is that? What kind of *person* is that?"

"Gracie, you had every reason to feel that way. Look at your childhood. And, anyway, that's just simply not true. I remember plenty of occasions when you were in awe of her. You're just choosing not to remember those because you feel bad."

"No, Finn," she said, convinced she was right. "I really don't remember a time that I didn't want to get away from that house. I blamed her for so much."

He was quiet, leaning back on the swing, stretching his leg out and pushing off it so they swayed back and forth again. "What about right after he left? I had dinner at your place a few nights after and you followed her around the house, the biggest smile on your face. It was like you knew she was free. Hannah accidentally burped at the table after dinner and your mama made this silly face, something I'd never seen her do before." He put his hands to his chest for effect. "By the time dessert came we were all trying to out-burp each other. You leaned over to me later, when we were watching TV, and you said 'Isn't she great? She's really somethin', isn't she?' and you kept saying it all night, like you were so proud of her."

Gracie tried to remember, but that was the thing about leaving your life behind. Some of your memories stayed back, too.

"And when I came to get you before senior prom? You poked your head out of your room, and yelled for her. Said she needed to see you first because mamas waited for this day, to see their little girls so grown up. That it was a moment for a mama and her daughter and I could just wait a bit longer." Gracie did remember that. Mama had walked down the hall, coming into her room and gasping, clamping her hand over her mouth before breaking into a big smile. Gracie had curtsied in her sparkling magenta dress, then spun around, twirling like a ballerina. She remembered the tears in Mama's eyes, and as she and Finn left to meet Olivia and Grant, she'd looked back as they drove down the street to see Mama watching them, still smiling that wide smile, a proud mother who then went to work her third double shift that week. Nine days later, Gracie missed her period and life as she knew it changed forever.

She closed her eyes as they swayed together, his arm draped across her shoulders.

"Is that how you remember everything?" he asked after a while. "Have you forgotten all the good things?"

"I don't know, Finn. I guess maybe it's painful to remember sometimes."

"It would make it easier to stay away, I guess."

She waited for him to say more, but he didn't, and she realized he didn't want to elaborate. Not here. Not on this day. So they rocked together, and Gracie, breathing in the moment, didn't try to remember or forget. She'd never been very good at either, anyway.

The wind was swirling outside her window, and Gracie shuddered upon hearing it, folding herself into the wool blanket around her shoulders. She walked over to it, peering through the darkness, looking for any sign of Finn. Her efforts were futile. She couldn't see a thing.

"Gracie?" Hannah asked from outside her door. "Can I come in?"

"Sure," she said, sitting down on her bed. When her sister entered she motioned for her to sit beside her. "What's up?"

"I've been talking with Mama," she said, her forehead wrinkling at whatever was on her mind. "You know, I'm only back for another few days before classes start up again."

"Mm-hmm."

"Well, I'm thinking of not going back."

"What?" Gracie asked, startled.

Hannah remained calm, while Gracie was anything but. "My student loans are atrocious."

"But, H. You've already got a year-and-a-half under your belt, why would you quit now?"

"I wouldn't quit, necessarily," she said, playing with a loose thread on her sweater. "I mean, I might go back eventually. I think it just makes more sense for me to help out here."

"And Mama's okay with this?" Gracie didn't know why, but she suddenly felt angry, like she was being let down.

"She said as much."

"But, H, don't you want to get out of here? Don't you want to *do* something with your life?"

"Of course I want to do something. And I will. But, Gracie..." Her voice quavered. "I've never felt the need to get out of here. I know you do. I know you and Finn are..."

"Don't make this about me and Finn. This is about you and me getting out of Glenwood. Both of us. I thought you wanted that."

"I thought I did, too. But Mama has no one. And I like it here. Can you honestly see me exploring some big city?

I visited some friends over in Ashland and I was like a duck out of water."

Gracie tried to wrap her mind around what Hannah was telling her. This wasn't the plan. *Their* plan. The plan they'd all talked about since they realized there was a whole world outside Glenwood. Hannah moved from the doorway and sat beside Gracie on the bed. She rubbed her hands together as if she were cold, and Gracie opened her arms wide, holding onto each end of the blanket. Hannah slid in beside her, wrapping herself up next to Gracie.

"Are you sure about this?" Gracie asked.

"I am. I can always go back."

Gracie sighed. Even she knew that was unlikely. If Hannah quit now, she'd probably be married within a year and working for pennies at whatever job opened up next in Glenwood.

"Things will be alright," Hannah said. Gracie wasn't sure if it was for her benefit that she said it, or her own. When she got up to leave a few minutes later, Gracie stopped her.

"You know this is why you've always been the favorite."

Hannah lifted an eyebrow.

"Yeah," Gracie continued. "You always put them first. Daddy, when he was still here, knew it. Mama knows it. It's why they adore you."

The words floated between them before Hannah's head fell. She shook it back and forth. "I wish you could see that I wasn't so different from you. We've both had expectations to live up to."

Before Gracie could respond, Hannah turned on her heel, her hair flowing behind her, leaving Gracie to her thoughts.

A few minutes later, Finn popped his head in. He had on his heavy Carhartt coat, and as he stepped into Gracie's room, he shook ice crystals from his head.

"Just showered," he said, grinning. "Man, it's cold out." He leaned down, kissing Gracie on the lips. When she didn't return the kiss, he frowned. "Everything okay?"

Gracie stood up, walking over to shut her bedroom door. "Not in the least."

Finn pulled off his coat and sat down where Gracie had been. "It's not something I did, is it?" he asked.

A smile spread across Gracie's face. "No." She walked back to the window, looking out at the darkness below. "H isn't going back to school."

"Well," he said. "School's not for everyone."

She whipped around. "But it's the ticket out of here."

"Not everyone wants to leave, Gracie."

"But Hannah did want to leave."

"Did she?" It was obvious he didn't think so.

"Didn't she?" Gracie asked, suddenly feeling less certain.

Finn got up from the bed, reaching his hands out to her. She took them, looking up into his eyes. "I never got the feeling that she did," he said, surprising her with his honesty. Gracie felt Finn's arms go around her, closing her in. She let herself nestle into the crook of his neck, taking in the smell of him, the feel of him. "I missed you today," he said. He hugged her close, for just a moment, then, letting go of her, got up and picked up his coat. "I brought you your Christmas present."

"Christmas isn't for two more days."

"It seems like you need a little cheering up." He reached into the pocket of his coat and pulled out a small box, wrapped in red paper and silver string. "Merry Christmas, Gracie."

She took the small gift in her hand, feeling it between her fingers. "Are you sure you want me to open it already?"

Before he could answer, there was a knock at the door. Hannah opened it, poking her head around it. "Mama just left and I'm going to go grab some dinner with Kim and Sammi. You two want to come?"

"No thanks," Gracie said. She knew she wouldn't be able to keep her opinions to herself, and right now, she needed to. Hannah would never listen to her if she tried bullying her into staying in school.

"Alright. Call me if you want me to bring something back."

"Sure." Hannah retreated, and the sound of the front door opening and closing a few seconds later left Gracie and Finn alone.

Gracie pulled on the string, untying the silver bow. Flipping open each side, she slid the box out of the wrapping. Finn watched her fingers move along the sides of the box. He cocked his head to look at her. "Are you going to open it?"

She smiled, nodding. Lifting the lid off, she looked down at her gift.

"Oh my God."

Finn smiled. "You like it," he said, matter-of-factly.

"Where did you get this?" she asked, stunned. "I figured Riley probably lost it years ago."

Finn reached in and pulled out the switchblade. "I asked him for it after he'd gotten his use out of it."

"You mean after he showed it off to absolutely anyone who'd listen to his crazy story."

Gracie took it in her hands, rubbing her fingers over the bright orange handle. The blade was folded into itself, and she triggered the flipper, letting it loose. "Why are you giving it to me?"

He stood up and walked to the window, where she had been standing moments ago. His expression thoughtful, he rubbed the back of his neck. "I had that blade for a long time. And I never could figure out what compelled me to keep it." He turned, looking at her with an intensity she knew well. Finn always looked at her that way, like every moment meant something. She was used to it by now, but it also had her retreating for reasons she didn't yet understand. When he spoke again, his voice was soft. "Then, I realized it was because I love you." He'd never said it out loud before, and Gracie looked away, unable to meet his eyes. "And I've loved you since that day. Well, it was probably well before that day, really. But, that day I knew it for sure."

"The day I kept calling you a wanker," Gracie whispered, a smile creeping across her face. She looked back at him, meeting his eyes.

Finn laughed out loud. "You did seem keen on that word, yeah." She pushed the blade down, securing it within the cover. "It was also the first time I remember feeling like I needed to protect you."

Gracie lifted an eyebrow. "Finn Miller, you know I don't need protecting."

"Ah," he said, shaking his head. "This I know. I guess I just mean, it was the first time I wanted to be the one to protect you."

Gracie nodded, understanding both his feelings that day and the sentiment behind the unusual gift. "We were just kids then," she said. He didn't say anything, but moved toward her. She stood, facing him. "Thank you."

"And don't worry about my gift. I know you're a last minute shopper." His eyes were twinkling, and his smile mischievous.

She set the blade down on the bed, then turned to Finn, forcing herself to look at him. She didn't know why it was so hard for her accept Finn's love. But she wanted to. Oh, how she wanted to. "I love you, too, you know." Finn bent down, cupping her head in his hands. When he kissed her, she felt her whole body relax and she whispered, softly, into his ear. "I want to be with you."

Finn stopped kissing her, straightening up so he was looking down at her. "You're sure?" he asked, knowing exactly what she meant. Gracie thought she'd never seen him so serious. "I've never wanted anything more, but I want you to be sure, Gracie, because once we do this, there's no turning back."

She wasn't sure what he meant by that, but she nodded anyway. "I know," she said, pulling him back down to her. "I'm sure."

When he kissed her again, it was hard and fast, as if he might lose her at any moment. She tugged at her top, pulling it over her head while he unzipped his pants. When they came together, he moved slowly, but she could feel the hunger radiating from him. His hands moved across her body so expertly she wondered if they had been destined for this all along. She'd never loved anyone else. Nor, she thought, would she. There was only Finn. And there only ever had been.

Later that night as she lay in bed, she remembered Finn's face as he dressed himself to go. "We're in this," he'd said before he'd left her room. And she knew they were. Their whole lives were ahead of them. Soon, they'd be accepting their diplomas and moving on, finally getting the hell out of Glenwood—together.

8.

GRACIE THREW THE LAST OF HER CLOTHES INTO THE
suitcase, zipping it shut without much trouble. She hadn't
packed much because she hadn't intended on being in
Glenwood for long, but that morning after she'd called her
boss to discuss how much longer she would be gone, she
realized she wasn't quite ready to say goodbye. Since
they'd just hired two new nurses who were eager to take
on extra shifts and learn the ropes, Gracie was allowed a
few extra days of leave.

Hannah had insisted on moving her into Cayla's room
for the remainder of her trip. At first, she'd declined, but
staying at the hotel an extra week would have been
stretching her monthly budget, and she wanted to spend
more time with Cayla.

"It's no problem at all, Gracie. Cayla can just bunk with
us for a few nights," Hannah had said. When Gracie
finally relented, accepting that she wouldn't be an
imposition, Hannah had immediately removed Cayla's
sheets to throw them in the wash and started setting out
extra towels.

"I'm not staying forever," she'd said. "I'll just need the
one towel."

Her sister had shrugged, a smile on her face. Gracie
knew what she was thinking. But Gracie wasn't going to
let herself get too comfortable in Glenwood. There were
too many memories. Too many people she'd let down.
Glenwood was like the favorite dress you had as a kid that

you wore to the park when you weren't supposed to. The one that now frayed at the bottom and had mud stains all over it, and whenever you went to pull it out of the closet, you remembered it was ruined, and that if you wore it again, everyone else would see it was ruined too. Gracie didn't mind people thinking she'd done something wrong, but she didn't want a lasting reminder of her bad choices following her around and mocking her incessantly.

She glanced up at the sound of her phone vibrating on the nightstand.

"Hey, Gracie," Hannah breathed into the phone.

"H, what's up?"

"Are you headed here yet?" Hannah sounded like she was in a hurry.

"Not yet. Just packing up the last of my stuff. Something wrong?"

There was a pause before Hannah answered. "No, nothing's wrong."

"H, what is it?"

"Oh, I just forgot about a meeting I had tonight. It's nothing. I'll just call and cancel it."

"I'm about to leave. What time is the meeting?"

"Six. Usually Dave's home by now, but he got stuck at work for longer than he thought and..." Hannah's voice trailed off.

Gracie looked at the clock. It was ten 'til. "I'll be there in five. Will that give you enough time?"

"Are you sure?" Hannah asked.

"Of course."

"Okay then. Yeah, it will be fine."

By the time Gracie got to the house, Hannah had about two minutes to get to her meeting. She was out the door as Gracie carried her suitcase across the front lawn. "So, where are you headed?" she asked.

Hannah waved her off. "Cayla's inside. It won't be more than an hour."

Gracie watched her sister leave, her curiosity piqued at the way Hannah had brushed off her question.

When she entered the house, she noticed right away that it was immaculate. Hannah had made sure of that. Cayla was in her room, dancing around in a pair of green fairy wings, holding a wand.

"I wish for my Aunt Gracie to kiss me," she said when she saw Gracie at the door.

Gracie bent down, kissing Cayla's cheek lightly. Cayla grinned from ear to ear.

"Why haven't I seen you before, Aunt Gracie?" she asked after twirling around the room again.

"Well," Gracie began, not sure exactly how to answer the question. Did she even have a good answer for her? Anything she said sounded ridiculous now when she thought about the fact that she'd missed out on Cayla's first years. "I just had to go away for a while."

"Why?"

"At the time, I guess I just thought I needed to," she said, sitting down on the edge of Cayla's bed.

Cayla stopped twirling. "Will you go away again?"

"I'll have to go back eventually. But I won't stay away this time, Cayla. I promise."

"With pinkies?" Cayla asked. She held out her hand waiting for Gracie to pinkie swear.

"With pinkies."

Cayla went back to twirling, her hair flowing behind her as she jumped around the room. "Where did my mom go?" she asked, looking over her shoulder.

"She said she had a meeting."

"With Dr. Taft?"

"Who's Dr. Taft?" Gracie asked, alarmed.

Cayla shrugged. "Mommy goes to her office sometimes."

It felt like all the air went out of the room at Cayla's declaration. Was Hannah sick? How would Cayla know the name of a doctor that Hannah just saw once a year for a checkup? And why did she call the appointment a meeting? Gracie tried to push the thoughts aside, but she was scared. She'd finally come home, and her mother was gone. She couldn't lose her sister, too.

"Cayla, how often does your mom see Dr. Taft?" she asked.

"I dunno."

"Does she take you to her office sometimes?"

"No. She says I'm too little."

Because Hannah didn't want to worry Cayla? Calm down, she told herself. Maybe it was just easier to leave Cayla behind.

By the time Dave got home, Gracie was trying to beat Cayla at Candyland (of which she'd already lost three games) while simultaneously trying not to believe any of the reasons popping into her head about why her sister would need to have regular appointments with Dr. Taft.

"I win again!" Cayla shouted. "I'm done playing this, Aunt Gracie. It's not really fun anymore."

Losing every game wasn't much fun, either, she thought. "That's fine," she said, watching Cayla run to her room.

"Dave?" She walked into the kitchen to find Dave reheating some of the food remaining from the barbecue the other night, before sitting down at the table.

"Hey, Gracie. Thanks for watching her tonight. I just couldn't get away." He took a bite. "Did you get settled in Cayla's room? Don't let her push you around. She's not used to sharing her space, but Hannah talked to her about it last night."

"Oh yeah. She helped me put things in an empty drawer of her dresser, actually." Gracie took a seat beside him at the table. "Can I ask you something?"

"Sure." He put his fork down and took a sip of the ice water in front of him.

"Who is Dr. Taft? Cayla mentioned her earlier."

He put his water down and looked at Gracie. "I'm not sure if it's my place to say," he said.

"She's not sick, is she?"

"No, she's not."

Gracie wasn't sure whether to believe him. She barely knew Dave. He could have been lying to protect Hannah. She didn't know what to believe. Before she could stop herself, she started to cry.

"Gracie," he said, reaching over to her awkwardly, trying to comfort her. "She's fine. Your sister is fine."

"Are you sure?"

"I'm sure." He scooted his chair closer to her. "Listen, I'll tell you who Dr. Taft is. I don't want you thinking she's got a terminal illness or something, and I can see you won't entirely believe me unless I do. Hannah'll kill me, but I think it's fair for you to know, and I can deal with her."

Gracie stopped crying, looking at this man, clearly wanting to appease the relative stranger in his kitchen, as well as his wife. She shouldn't be putting him in such a position, but she had to know.

"Dr. Taft is Hannah's therapist."

"Her therapist?" Gracie spit the word out, each consonant amplified as it rolled off her tongue.

"Yes," he said, before coughing to clear his throat. "She started seeing her before we met. She's gone to her religiously every other week for years."

"But Hannah's so together. She doesn't seem like she needs a therapist."

Dave shook his head. "She doesn't talk about it much. And don't take this the wrong way, Gracie, but I think she took it pretty personally when you left."

Gracie's mouth fell open. She knew what she'd done affected other people, but she never thought in a million years it would cause Hannah so much distress. And anyway, they had kept in touch through email. But even as Gracie went over their interactions in her mind, she knew it wasn't enough. They'd been close. Hannah had loved her as much as their mother had. In some ways, she may have loved her more.

Dave patted her on the shoulder. "Hey, it's alright. This is a new start. People start over all the time. While she's upset about your mother, we've had time to plan for that." Gracie kept forgetting that everyone else had known about her mother's illness. "She's thrilled to have you back. Truly. I've never seen her so happy." He stood up, taking his plate to the sink, then turned back to Gracie. "We're all glad you're here, Gracie."

She forced a smile and watched Dave go into the living room. She should've felt reassured by Dave's words, but all she felt was empty.

"You're getting better," Gracie said, reaching down to tie her shoelace. She tugged on it, looping the ends of the shoelace and pulling it tight before crossing her legs and leaning back on her hands.

"You practice as much as I do and you'd get better, too."

"I don't want to learn how to play that thing."

"Why not?" Finn asked, resting the guitar on his knee. "We could be like Sonny and Cher."

"I'd like to see you with that hairdo," Gracie said, squinting from the sun. "Plus, if I'm playing guitar, how am I going to help you improve?"

"What? You mean by telling me every time I play the wrong note?"

Gracie smiled seductively. "Exactly. I'm going to make you a star, Finn. Can't have me goin' and stealin' your spotlight."

Finn chuckled, knowing Gracie's debilitating fear of being on stage. He'd tried to pull her on stage just last month at one of their local gigs and she hadn't spoken to him for a week after, huffing away in indignation. She and Tucker had that in common.

He set the guitar down and reached for her. "More like, can't have you distracting me every second with your feminine wiles."

"My what?" Gracie wrinkled up her nose. "I'm fairly certain I have none of *those*."

Finn laughed as he always did when Gracie acted like he was crazy for being attracted to her. He pulled her to him again. She smiled and leaned down to kiss him.

"What are you workin' on now, anyway? You guys going to write some actual songs, finally?"

He shrugged. "I don't know. We're just doin' it for fun. It's not like we'll be doing this ten years from now."

"Maybe you will," Gracie said, watching him. "It seems like it means something to you. I mean, you really have gotten into it, haven't you?"

"I guess so," he said. "I like singing other people's songs. I like hearing the crowd sing along with me."

"But if you write some stuff, they'll sing *your* words, won't they?"

"Well, yeah. I guess I just haven't known what to write." He trailed his finger down the side of her face. "What would you write?"

"Probably some sad song about a dog and a cornfield."

Finn rolled his eyes. "Just because we *are* country, doesn't mean we have to *be* country."

Gracie sighed. "I don't know. I guess maybe something similar to Shawn Colvin."

"Oh, Gracie..." Finn's head rolled back, remembering all the times she'd played "Never Saw Blue Like That" on repeat.

"What?" She laughed, nudging him with her arm. "She's great!"

"You know, deep down, you *are* just like other girls."

"What's that mean?"

"Just that you like all that sappy stuff."

"Well, if good songwriting is what you describe as sappy, then yes, I guess I *am* a girl."

He laughed. "Yes, you are. My girl."

She kissed him again. "Now, there's a good song."

"Not quite what the great Shawn Colvin would sing, though."

Gracie scowled. "They're each great in their own badass epic song way. Anyway, I think I've given you some good things to think about. This was a good meeting."

"Oh, so now our time together is as artist and manager?" He pulled away, letting his body fall back onto the grass.

"No," she said, lying back with him. A little while later, still thinking, she added, "But really, Finn, you should write something."

"Okay," he said, long after she'd said it. "Maybe, someday, I will."

9.

GRACIE TOOK A SEAT IN THE CORNER OF THE BAR. IT WAS A successful night by anyone's standards. The room was full of patrons, and Gracie looked over her shoulder, looking for Olivia and Grant. As the minutes passed, it became more and more apparent they wouldn't be there to keep her company. While she'd promised Finn she'd come watch the show, now she felt out of place, sitting on her own. Her first drink was almost gone, and her nerves were getting the best of her. She felt like she was the one about to get on stage any minute.

A few minutes later when she saw Finn walk out with Tucker, Will and Ty, she realized what it was. Finn spotted her immediately. He nodded in her direction. She remembered listening as he learned to play. His fingers had strummed chords meticulously, day after day, trying to teach them where to go until one day his clumsy, faltering hands were eventually replaced by graceful ones.

"Thank you all for coming tonight," he said as he adjusted his guitar strap. There were a few hollers from the audience, and Finn paused, letting them die down. "Some of you may have seen us play before. If you've been to one of our shows, you'll know I always start each one with the same song." He paused, then looked back in Gracie's direction. "This song is very personal to me. I wrote it for someone—well, my best friend, in fact. And she's here tonight." He moved his eyes away from her when he said it, so as not to give her away, then turned to

Tucker and nodded, before moving back to the microphone. "This is 'Gracie's Song'."

As the music filled the room, Gracie realized she was holding her breath. And as he started to sing, he looked to her once more, then closed his eyes as the first words filled the room.

> Remember chasing fireflies
> My heart entwined with yours
> 'Til something in your face changed, I didn't recognize
> We weren't meant to be
>
> I never expected you to go
> If you come back, promise to stay with me now
> Before I sink in these waters so deep below
> Where it's just you and me
>
> I wish for a place that's a memory
> It makes me weary, girl
> Thinking of your face, the only face I see
> Winding through and through this lifeless place
>
> And wherever you might be walking, do you see me there?
> I think I see you everywhere
> I'd know that blush anywhere
> I've fallen down under the ol' willow tree
> You remember us there?—I know you do, I know you do
> Watching the sun go down, living our dreams out loud
> And we weren't afraid in those days,
> you and me
>
> I wait for you, take me back to that time
>
> I wait for the day you come back to me
>
> Oh, you went away
>
> And I wait for the day you come back to me

Gracie stared at the stage. The pain in his words ambushed her. She didn't know whether to smile or cry. Part of her wanted to get up and run out of the place, and not face what she was feeling, but she wouldn't do it. She'd done enough running for a lifetime. Instead, she turned and ordered another drink as Finn started in on the next song, but it was the words from his first that lingered in her ear for the rest of the night.

"Having fun?" he asked as he slipped in beside her.

She smiled, not looking at him right away. "I am, actually."

"I knew you would."

She turned to set her drink down, lifting her eyes to him. "Finn, that song..." Her voice trailed off and she looked away.

"Which song is that?" Her eyes moved back to his face. He was smiling, teasing her.

"When did you write it?"

He shrugged. "Not long after you left."

"You've been singing that at every show since I left?"

He nodded. "First song at every show. Tuck says it's about time I retire it, but I don't know. It's kind of our trademark now."

"It was beautiful."

The bartender brought Finn a drink on the house. He took a long sip from the glass, cocking his head back and closing his eyes. When he set it down again, it was only half full. He took a deep breath, then put a hand over hers. "I'm really glad you liked it, Gracie." They stared at each other, caught up in the moment. Finally, Finn picked up his drink again and stood up. "Well, I've got to play another set."

"Oh, sure."

He looked around. "Grant and Olivia didn't make it?"

"I guess not," she said, shrugging.

"Well, I understand if you need to go. It'll be a late night for me here."

Gracie nodded, standing up to go.

"Meet me tomorrow morning," he said, looking back as the others made their way to the stage.

"Where?"

"Our old neighborhood."

"Okay. What time?"

"Ten okay?"

"Sure," she said.

"Don't forget, now," he said, before turning to walk back to the stage. "I'm counting on you."

And that's exactly what Gracie was afraid of.

Gracie made her way out of the bar and into the quiet night outside. There was a full moon, lighting up the street more than the flickering streetlights that lit the way back to her car. As she stepped off the curb to cross the street, she heard a voice from behind her. "Gracie Brannen."

She turned around to see him leaning against the building she'd just exited. "Nick Tooley," she said, her curiosity piqued.

Gracie waited for him to say something, but he simply continued to stare at her until, frustrated, she asked him, "What are you doing here?"

"I wanted to talk to you." His voice was deeper than she'd anticipated and it took her by surprise.

"About?"

"Your mother, of course." He took a step toward her so that he was no longer leaning back. Gracie took a step away from him.

"What *was* your relationship with my mother, anyway?" Just because Hannah had been too polite to ask didn't mean she was going to be.

"What do you think?"

Gracie shrugged, then crossed her arms in front of her. "My sister thinks you dated." He laughed at that. She frowned, annoyed. "So, you didn't?"

"No," he said. "I'm a little young, aren't I?"

"I'd say so. How old are you?"

"Thirty-five."

A door opened to the bar next to them and a group of people crowded onto the sidewalk, laughing and shouting. Two tipsy girls linked arms and started singing "Sweet Home Alabama" as they walked in the opposite direction of Gracie and Nick. Both of them watched as the group grew smaller in the distance.

"Would you come with me?" Nick asked, turning to face her again.

"I don't even know you."

"But your mother did."

"Mama never told me about you."

He didn't say anything for a moment, then looked at his feet, and up again, resolved to say whatever it was he was contemplating in his head. "Well, you weren't really here for her to tell you, now were you?"

Gracie's mouth fell open. "You have no right to..."

"To what? Say the truth? I knew Sarah well. Probably better than you."

Gracie felt the heat come to her cheeks. She put her hands on her hips and stomped her foot as if that might force the anger from her body. This man—this boy, really —had no right to say these things to her. "Excuse me? What do you know about it?" Then, not wanting to know his answer, she proceeded to drop her hands and ball up her fists in frustration. "I don't have to listen to the likes of you. I don't even *know* you."

Nick just stared at her, as if he were waiting for her outburst to be over. It was then that she recognized him. The look on his face at that moment. It came at her like a bolt of lightning, striking her paralyzed, causing her to refocus on her surroundings.

"You're him," she whispered.

He waited.

"You were there that day at the fair. Watching us."

He didn't deny it, just kept watching her.

"Who are you, Nick Tooley?"

"Come with me, and I'll tell you."

She hesitated, but pulled out her keys. "Where?"

He turned. "That's my car there," he said, pointing to a blue sedan up the street. "Follow me."

He walked away then, slowly making his way to his vehicle. Gracie unlocked her car and sat down in the driver's seat. Should she call Hannah? It was getting late and she still had to drive back. She pulled out her phone and started typing out a text as Nick's headlights went on. *Ran into Nick. Stopping somewhere for a chat then I'll be on my way. G*

She followed him to a diner halfway between Glenwood and Ashland. They sat down in a corner booth, Nick ordering a decaf coffee. "And what would you like, dear?" the bottle-blonde waitress asked.

"Nothing for me," she said.

The waitress—Eileen—put her hand on her hip. Gracie took that to mean she wasn't impressed with serving a coffee drinker and non-eater this late at night. "I'll bring some menus."

"So," Gracie said once Eileen had brought Nick's cup of coffee, setting it and the menus on the table in front of them. "What are we doing here?"

Nick took a sip, then set the cup down and clasped his hands together. "This here is where I first met your mom."

Gracie looked around. It was small, a little less clean than she would have liked if she was a regular here, but it had an old-school charm about it. "When?"

"It was right around the time she'd been diagnosed." Hannah had told her it was a year ago. That, at first, they'd thought she'd have more time.

"Were you both eating here?" she asked, confused.

"Oh no. We'd planned to meet here," Nick said. He took another sip of coffee, then made a face, set the cup down and grabbed a sugar packet from the middle of the table, pouring it into the cup and stirring it around with his spoon. "She'd just found out about the cancer when she called me."

Gracie felt her heart plummet. Instead of contacting her daughter, her mother had called this guy? She wanted to be furious, and she was, but she was also reminded that it was her fault. "How did she sound?"

"She sounded okay, Gracie. I mean, it was the first time I'd ever talked to her before so I had no way to know."

"What did she want? She just called you out of the blue?"

He nodded. "She must've been doing some digging. I mean, months or years prior to actually calling me. As we talked it became apparent that she'd been putting it off, but that something had made her reach out to me."

"Her diagnosis."

"Yes."

Eileen came back and pulled out her pad of paper. "You change your mind?" she asked, though it didn't sound exactly like a question.

Gracie sighed and flipped open the menu. "Just bring me some fries."

"Just fries?"

"Yep."

Eileen wrote something down on the pad. It could have been fries, but Gracie didn't know why anyone would need to write that down. "What about you?" she asked Nick, still frowning at Gracie.

"Oh, um, how about a Reuben? And a side of mashed potatoes?" Eileen perked right up. "Oh, and a root beer."

"I'll bring that right out, honey," Eileen said, batting her heavily mascaraed eyelashes at Nick, who had just become her new favorite customer. She didn't look back at Gracie before she headed back to the kitchen.

"You're going to eat all that now?"

"I felt bad for her," Nick said.

"She was rude," Gracie countered, angry that she was even in this restaurant at all.

"So were you."

"She never saw you at the fair," Gracie said, changing the subject. "Only Daddy and I did."

"I know. But some things have a way of comin' out."

"Things like..."

"The fact that she found me makes me think she knew my mom." Nick stirred his coffee again, but didn't bring it to his mouth to take another sip, instead just watching the liquid move around the spoon's handle.

"Your mama work with her?"

"No."

"Look, Nick, just tell me what's going on. You're running me in circles and I'm getting to the point where I'm not going to care *how* you knew my mom. I'm just going to want to leave."

Nick looked at her as if she'd just said her hair was on fire. "You've got quite a temper, and you're not very nice, Gracie Brannen."

She didn't respond.

"Okay," he said, sitting back in the booth. "Remember that day at the fair? You and your old man were just dandy, playin' games, winnin' prizes." Gracie didn't mention that her dad was on his way to passing out on the living room floor. "I had been walking up the midway and finally found him. I knew him right away. But it was you that kept me lookin' and you that kept me standin' still. You see, I'd finally found out who he was, and I'd been waitin' for the right time to tell him off."

Gracie sat back, suddenly realizing where this story was going. She should have known. The similarities were astounding, but Gracie always pictured her father as the unkempt drunkard that he was. If Nick didn't have that silly mustache, and her daddy had taken care of himself, they'd look pretty close to identical. "He was your daddy, too," she whispered.

"Sperm donor is more like it."

"You never saw him?"

"Up until I was about three he lived with us. Then took off. Must've come to Glenwood and met your Ma."

"Well, if it makes you feel better, he was a terrible father."

"It doesn't make me feel better," he said, offended. "Like I said, I went there to tell him off, but then I saw you. You seemed happy—at least in that moment. And I couldn't do it. I thought, maybe he's changed, maybe he's started over and is doing things right. He saw me, too, then and that was enough. He knew I knew what he'd done."

"And Mama figured all this out?"

"Maybe she knew all along."

"But why'd she want to talk to you?"

"Your ma," he put a hand through his hair and a smile broke out across his face as he remembered her. "She was a sweet woman. When we met here way back, she said I didn't deserve what happened to me. She wanted me to know what he was like. She said I escaped a hellish thing, having him for a father."

Gracie thought about this for a moment, trying to picture her parents, together, but those memories were fuzzy. She'd tried to block them out, and they'd faded more and more as time passed. "Did she say why she stayed with him, then?"

"She said she was weak. That she hoped he would change. All the stuff you hear people say all the time about bad relationships." Nick took another sip of his coffee. "She never asked about my mom. She just wanted me to know that I was better off. If she'd asked, she would've known my mom died when I was sixteen, before that day I saw you at the fair. But she didn't ask, so I didn't tell. After that day, we kept meeting up. Always in different places. Eventually, she invited me over for dinner with your sister's family. She didn't want Hannah to know, but she wanted me to meet her."

"Why?"

"She said Hannah was dealing with a lot. I mean, she'd just found out about the cancer. She never talked about you, which worried your ma. There was Cayla."

"So Hannah's left to think you're Mama's new boy toy."

Nick laughed, pushing his sleeves up on his arms. "I suppose she just wanted Sarah to be happy, and to Hannah that meant finding love again."

That actually made sense.

Eileen returned, setting Nick's meal down in front of him.

"Thank you," he said, giving her a gratuitous smile.

"You're so welcome, dear," she said. Then, her smile disappearing, she turned to Gracie. "I'll be right back with your fries."

When she came back with the plate, she set it down and quickly turned around.

"Uh, ketchup?" Gracie asked as Eileen walked away.

"On the table." She didn't even turn around.

"Five-star service at this place, huh?" she said, rolling her eyes. Nick handed her the ketchup.

"You could've just been nice to her."

"And order a second dinner like you did? I'm not even hungry." She squirted the middle of the bottle, watching it ooze out into a red clump on the side of her plate. The fries were typical diner fries, crinkly, crispy and greasy as all get out. Once Gracie popped one in, she ate the rest just because they were there, and because fries taste damn good after you've had a few drinks.

When they'd eaten most of their food, Gracie sat back, thinking. "What's the point in telling me all of this? I understand why Mama didn't want Hannah to know, but why tell me? Why now?"

"I suppose it's kind of selfish, but I wanted to know you. I was really curious. And, you leaving everyone behind...it seemed to me like you deserted everybody just like your old man did."

Gracie supposed it probably did look like that to him, and she didn't like the comparison one bit. "So? Now you've met me."

"So I have. Your ma always said you weren't to blame. She said you had your reasons and that she wasn't that great of a mother to you, letting you grow up in the household you did." He wiped his mouth with his napkin, then folded it up into a little ball and tossed it onto the table. "I guess I just wanted to see if she was right."

"And was she?"

"I don't know. It's too early to tell. You're not the warmest person I've ever met, but then, I sort of snuck up on you tonight. I don't blame you for being on edge."

"Were you in the bar earlier?"

He nodded.

"How long?"

"Long enough to hear that guy sing about you." Nick studied her. "Who was he, anyway?"

"That's none of your business," Gracie's face grew hot, and she crossed her arms in front of her. Then, seeing Nick studying her, she added. "We grew up together."

"He still loves you?"

Gracie shrugged. "I haven't seen him in almost ten years."

"Well, it seems that you left quite a mess behind when you left, which means you can't be all that bad. If all these people were so balled up when you left, there has to be a reason."

Gracie didn't know what to say.

"I think maybe your ma was right. Maybe I did escape him. But I've been on my own for a while now, and all I know is it can get lonely. Now, you're back, and I'm just wonderin' if you felt that way, too—bein' away."

Nick reached back for his wallet, then threw a bunch of bills down on the table. "This'll cover everything."

"You don't have to pay for me," Gracie said, pulling out her wallet.

"You don't think I can afford an extra plate of fries?" He winked at her, and she smiled. It must have surprised him because he stopped what he was doing and just looked at her for a long time.

"I decided it was time I stopped bein' lonely," he said, finally.

They got up to go, Nick waving at Eileen as they left. Gracie stopped once they were outside, and turned to him.

"I do feel that way," she said, tucking her hair behind her ears. "Sometimes, I think I've screwed everything up."

"I don't think so."

"I have, Nick. I really have."

"Everything can be undone. You can always find a way back." He smiled at her again, then turned and walked to his car. "Night, Gracie."

"Goodnight," she heard herself answer.

Gracie watched him drive off. Did she want to find a way back? Could she salvage her relationship with her sister? What about Finn? Now, there was Nick—a brother she never knew she had. And instead of hugging him and being grateful to him for giving her this information—an insight into her mother's last year, she had been rude to him, offended by him.

Everything can be undone.

Those words were why when she turned around, she didn't go to her car, but walked back into the diner to lay a twenty on their yet-to-be-cleared table.

The sobs awoke Gracie with a start. She listened through the walls, waiting for them to subside, but instead a rustling of sheets and footsteps down the hall brought her from Cayla's bedroom. The faucet was running in the kitchen, and a light had been turned on. She peeked around the corner to see Cayla at the table, her head in her hands. Hannah set a glass of water in front of her, but she didn't look up.

She didn't want to intrude, but found herself creeping slowly into the kitchen as Hannah sat down beside her daughter, putting a hand on her shoulder. Cayla continued to weep.

"I think she had a nightmare," Hannah whispered, spotting her.

Gracie moved into the room, taking a seat beside her sister. She glanced up at the clock on the stove. It read 3:11. "Poor thing," she said.

"Sorry she woke you. I tried to get her out here to calm her down where she wouldn't disturb you."

"Don't worry about it," Gracie said. "You forget I'm usually awake at this hour."

Cayla rubbed at her eyes, then yawned.

"Everything okay, honey?" Hannah asked her. Cayla looked up, unsure.

"I saw Grammy Sarah," she said. "She was in my dream. I wanted to give her a hug, but when I tried to, I woke up. I just want to give her a hug, Mama." The dimly lit kitchen seemed to cast shadows all around them. It made the room seem full, like the three of them sitting around the table weren't the only ones there.

"Oh," Hannah said. "I want to give Grammy a hug, too." There were tears in her eyes when she said it and it seemed to Gracie that she struggled to choke out the words.

Cayla reached for her glass, taking a long sip from it. When she'd finished, she yawned again and Gracie felt compelled to hold the child.

"I know it's not the same, but how about a hug from me?" Gracie asked. Cayla nodded, setting her cup down on the table and hopping off her chair. Gracie opened her arms, lifting her up and snuggling her close. She breathed in the sweet strawberry-flavored shampoo Hannah had used on her hair hours before. It reminded Gracie of Mama's garden. As kids, she and Hannah would sneak strawberries whenever Mama wasn't looking, leaving her frustrated and brainstorming ways to keep out the rabbits and squirrels.

As Cayla nestled into her arms, Gracie hummed softly, lulling her back to sleep. Hannah watched them, silently taking in the scene before her.

"Does she wake up like this often?" Gracie asked after a while, her voice hushed as Cayla slept in her arms.

Hannah shook her head. "There was a short time she did. She was around three years old then, I think. It was right after our dog, Chewy, ran off. But, otherwise, no. It's just been since Mama passed."

"They must have been very close."

"They were." Hannah said, resting her head on her hand, leaning into the table. She looked tired and Gracie wondered if she should let her go back to bed. "You know, I think Mama tried to do better by her. She wasn't working so hard, just taking care of herself, and they spent a lot of time together. Mama would take her over to Ashland from time to time. They'd go shopping or if some kind of festival was going on they'd go listen to the music and walk around to all the booths. Mama really made an effort with her, and I can't explain it, but there was a deep connection there. Ever since Cayla was born."

Gracie tried to remember her mother that way, but growing up they'd never done anything like what Hannah was saying. "I'm glad that she and Mama had that," Gracie said.

"Me too."

The ceiling fan was on, and Gracie watched it turning, feeling her eyes droop from looking at it. The blades were their only source of coolness, and Gracie was glad for it, Cayla's body a ball of heat on her lap.

"It must be hard for her to understand," she said, adjusting herself in her seat so she could better hold Cayla's weight.

"It's hard for me to even understand," Hannah replied, shaking her head. "I can't explain it to her in any way that makes sense. She asks me why her Grammy had to go away and I don't know what to say. Because I don't know why."

Gracie nodded.

"All I want to do is comfort her, but she's old enough now to understand that there are things in this life that are inexplicable. That there are no answers for some questions. That's a hard thing to accept."

"Something we all try to do our whole lives," Gracie added. "Can't expect a six-year-old to do it."

"Exactly."

The night before she had watched Cayla as she tried to catch fireflies in the front yard. With all the energy she could muster, she lunged at them, clapping her hands together and peeking through the cracks in her fingers to see if she'd caught one. Watching her, Gracie could picture Rosie there, running through the long blades of grass that hadn't been mowed for days, laughing with her cousin and waving to her on the porch. When she saw Rosie like that, as if she were still here, she was hit by her death all over again. It was a testament that however you learned to cope, grief could strike at any time, and especially when you least expected it.

Hannah got up from her chair, the strings of her bathrobe dragging along behind her. She reached up into one of the cupboards and pulled down a glass, then turned to look at Gracie. "Water?" she asked.

"Sure," she said, and Hannah reached for another.

She filled them up, above half-full and brought them to the table.

"How did you cope after Rosie?" Hannah asked, softly. She kept her eyes on the table as she sat down, and Gracie thought she might be too uncomfortable with her question to look up, but then she did, meeting Gracie's eyes.

It was a hard question to answer. In some ways, Gracie hadn't coped at all.

"I lost myself, H. There were months, years even, where I didn't know what I was doing. I think I walked through my life for a very long time, wondering how it had come to this. Wishing for things to be different. I blamed everyone else for what had happened to me. I blamed Daddy for runnin' off. I blamed him for stayin' so long and makin' us miserable. I blamed Finn for wanting more of his life. I blamed Mama for not being there, even though I hadn't let her. I blamed you, even. For coming home to Glenwood, and just falling in line with what everyone expected of our family by not getting out." She paused, taking a drink from her cup. "But, I blamed myself more than anyone else. For leaving. And for being so damn scared of everything."

Hannah was quiet. She looked over at her baby girl, whose legs were almost touching the floor now, lying in Gracie's arms. Rosie would have been around three years older than Cayla, which amazed her. While Hannah felt like time had gone by so fast, it had probably gone faster for Gracie, who had gone through all those years without watching her daughter grow.

"I see her sometimes," Gracie said, hugging Cayla to her.

"What do you mean?"

"Sometimes I can picture her as a little girl. I can see her as if she's with us somehow, watching us." She thought again of the other night, Cayla grasping at fireflies.

"And that's comforting?"

Gracie didn't have to think about the answer. "It is."

It wasn't like she was pretending that Rosie wasn't dead. She knew that her daughter was no longer here, in any real sense. What she felt in those rare and fleeting moments was a wanting, a desire for a memory that would never be real.

"I imagine that it would be," Hannah agreed.

After a while, the two women headed back down the hall, Gracie handing Cayla over to Hannah, before turning back down the hallway to Cayla's room.

"Goodnight," Hannah whispered.

"Night," Gracie said, her voice low. She sank back onto the bed, her head melting into the pillow. She closed her eyes and whispered into the night. "Goodnight, Rosie."

10.

THE SMELL OF COTTON CANDY FILLED THE AIR. GRACIE FELT her mouth fill with saliva as she inhaled the aroma. She looked over at her father, who sipped on his beer. He whistled through the small opening in his mouth, where the creases in his skin prominently came together to form a circle for the sound. He was in a good mood tonight. Leading Gracie and Hannah through the crowd, he linked his arm with their mother's. Screams came from the tilt-a-whirl. Gracie accidentally bumped into a carnie. He turned, his face painted like a clown and a cigarette hanging out of his mouth. Gracie looked away, the image a horrifying yet appropriate one for the setting. The carnie smiled and blew smoke in her direction. She raced ahead to catch up with the rest of her family as they slowly made their way through the crowd and she was thankful to no longer be looking into his bleary eyes. Her mother had a corndog in her hand and fed a bite to her father.

"Now that's fair food," he said, chomping down on it. Hannah was relaxed, sipping on a slushie. When her shoulders weren't tight with tension as they usually were around their father, she could have been almost normal. Gracie went to stand by her, keeping her eyes on their parents.

"You think he's gonna last like this all night?" Gracie asked.

Hannah nodded. "He likes the fair. I think he'll do alright." She was almost 13, and she looked older than her years. Gracie, who felt too young in her body, had spent the last few weeks envious of her big sister, and the accompanying attention she received from the boys (and men, if she was being honest) around them. Her father had noticed it, too, and he paraded her around, proud to show her off. While Gracie didn't like that one bit, she found herself wishing she wasn't so much younger. With each day, Hannah was closer to getting out of their house, while she was closer to being left behind. And the last thing she wanted was to be left behind.

They continued walking, stopping to talk to the Delores family, who went to their church. They had a son named Cap who was a year older than Hannah. He always looked at her with roving eyes, and it made Gracie want to kick in his goofy Coke-bottle glasses so he wouldn't be able to stare at her like that. Hannah pretended not to notice, or maybe she didn't notice. Gracie shouldn't have noticed either. She was too young to be thinking about such things, but she had Finn to thank for that. "Your sister's really pretty," he'd said one day as they climbed the treehouse.

"Oh yeah? Well, you can't have her, so why don't you keep it to yourself?"

"I don't want her. I'm just sayin'. I've seen lotsa boys lookin' at her lately, and ya know. I hear 'em talk."

For the first time, Gracie had looked at Hannah as others might have seen her and realized just how beautiful she was. To her, Hannah had always just been her big sister. It pissed her off to suddenly have to look at her as something else, apart from her.

"Girls, how 'bout you run over to the red tent over there and get me another Pabst?" The beer connoisseur. That was her father. "Here's a little extra money for something for yourselves." He thrust some bills at them. Hannah took them but looked concerned.

"Daddy," Hannah said, looking at him innocently. "We can't buy it. We're underage."

But their father was focused on their mother now and ignored her.

"We'll find somebody to get it for us," Gracie said.

The two girls made their way toward the red tent.

"Gracie!"

She turned to see Olivia standing near the tent. "Olivia, what are you doing?"

"Pat's playing in the band," she pointed to the stage where her older brother was playing the drums. Olivia had two older brothers. Pat was 21 and back for the summer to work with his father on the farm. Her other brother, Tristan, was 16 and the troublemaker of the family, in Gracie's opinion. "He said they're about to finish a set so I needed to wait for him right here. Then he said he'd take me on some rides.

"Can he buy Daddy a beer?" Hannah asked.

Olivia shrugged. "I'm not sure. I don't think he's old enough, but maybe." They waited for him to finish playing, and watched as he got off the stage and chatted to two girls who'd been dancing around the front of the crowd. When he finally made his way over, he winked at Hannah before turning to Olivia. "You ready, kid?"

"Oh yeah, but Pat, can you do something for Hannah and Gracie?"

"I can't take you all on the rides. Sorry." He looked annoyed.

"No," Olivia said, pointing to the red tent. "Can you get them a beer?"

"Aren't you a little young?" he asked Hannah.

"It's not for me," she replied, her mouth turned up in disgust. "It's for our dad."

"Oh. He still drinkin'? Man, that guy is a..." He stopped himself when he saw Hannah's face.

"He'll go batshit crazy if we come back empty-handed," Gracie whined.

"Don't he know the laws?"

"Our Daddy's a drunk, not an officer of the law," Gracie spat at him.

"Gracie," Hannah shushed her. "It's not his problem. We'll find someone else to do it."

"He'll get after ya if ya don't do it?" Pat asked, focused on Hannah, his voice turning sympathetic.

She nodded.

"Alright. I'll have one of my buddies do it."

They watched him walk away and when he came back, he handed them a plastic cup.

"Bye Olivia. Thanks for helping us." Gracie waved to her friend and watched as she and Pat made their way to the Ferris wheel. She and Hannah found their way back to their father, who was cheering loudly as his skee ball went into the smallest hole. "That right there's how you do it!" When he spotted Hannah with his drink, his face broke out into an even bigger smile. "Just in time, girls. Which one of ya wants to pick a prize?"

"Gracie can pick," Hannah answered.

"What'll it be, Gracie?" he asked, drinking half the cup in one gulp.

Gracie pointed to a stuffed pink dog, and her father handed it to her. It smelled like smoke and funnel cakes, but Gracie didn't care. It wasn't often her father gave her something. Hannah walked alongside their mother, towards another game, but Gracie was distracted by a boy watching her from across the midway. She held on tighter to the pink dog. He looked a few years older than Hannah, and there was something familiar about him, but Gracie knew she'd never seen him before. Her father, who'd been boasting about his win to the carnie, turned to her. "You got glue stuck to the bottom of your shoes, girl? Let's git a move on." When she didn't respond, her father followed her gaze.

"Who's that, Daddy?" she asked, not looking away from the boy.

Her father didn't answer, causing Gracie to look up at him. His face had turned white. She looked back at the boy who just stared at them until he quickly turned on his heel and disappeared into the crowd.

"Who was that?" she repeated.

Her father took the last sip of his drink, then put a hand on Gracie's shoulder. "Time to git," he said.

They left the fair after he'd herded up Mama and Hannah. Her sister had been wrong about that night. It ended up being one of his worst in a while. Hannah seemed surprised by it, but Gracie knew it was because of the boy.

"So, I wanted to show you something," Nick said as Gracie got into the squad car.

"We can drive around in this when you're off duty?" she asked, pulling on her seatbelt and simultaneously adjusting the AC.

"Well, I just got off work, and this won't take long." Gracie looked over at Nick, who was still wearing his uniform. She watched him—her brother—this strange creature who kept causing her to do double takes with his movements. She felt accustomed to him even though she didn't know him. It felt bizarre, yet oddly comforting as well. He put the car in reverse and pulled out of Hannah's driveway.

"So where is everyone?" he asked.

"Some church thing."

"And you didn't want to go?"

"I think at this point I'd rather not get pulled into the awkward conversations that would come with it."

Nick chuckled, adjusting his sunglasses as he drove. "I suppose that doesn't sound like such a fun time."

"So, where are we going?" she asked as they headed out of Glenwood.

"I told you. I just want to show you something."

Gracie waited for him to say more. Sensing her eyes on him, he turned to her. "It's not far. Really."

"But is it safe?" she asked. "That's the real question."

"Of course. Why wouldn't it be?"

"Well, you're basically a stranger to me."

"Basically," he said, mocking her. "Who just happens to share half your DNA." Gracie made a face at him, then realized the irony of the sibling-like gesture. "I've heard so much about you...from your ma, I mean. Guess I feel like I know you."

"But *I* don't know you. Haven't heard a word about you."

"Well, you're with me now. What do you want to know?"

Gracie shrugged. She had a lot of things she wanted to ask Nick, but it seemed strange to ask someone you barely knew about your own parents so she didn't respond. When they reached their destination twenty minutes later, arriving in the even smaller town of Wurley, Nick rolled to a stop and shut off the engine.

"See that house there?" Nick asked, pointing out the windshield to a small shanty-like structure across the street.

"Yeah."

"That's where I used to live."

Nick opened his door and stepped out of the car. Gracie did the same, though she wondered if Nick would want her to go inside the house, which sounded less than appealing. He must have sensed her reluctance because then he said, "Don't worry. I won't make you go in." He pulled out a cigarette and lit it.

"You smoke?" she asked, surprised.

"Only when I come back here," he said. He put it to his lips and inhaled, then breathed out again. "Gets to me."

"So why'd you bring me here then?"

He shrugged. "I don't know." He took another drag on his cigarette then dropped it to the ground and snuffed it out with his shoe. "My ma did her best. She did." He sat down on the curb in front of the car. Gracie went and sat down beside him. "I gotta say, though. Yours did a bit better."

"I didn't always think very highly of her."

"Yeah, well, it's nothin' to hate on your parents when you're a kid."

"Guess ours just made it easy."

"You know, when I lived there, we had a dirt floor in one of the bedrooms."

"No..."

Nick nodded. "Wore the same four shirts to school all year long 'til I was old enough to work and buy my own. Hardly had more than a few boxes of ramen to choose from to eat."

Uncomfortable, Gracie looked at her feet. "Why are you telling me this?"

"Because it's me. It's my life. And you're, somehow, connected to it."

"He wasn't there for you, was he?"

"It's done. No point in dwelling on it." He let out a whistle through his front teeth, then shook his head like he was fed up. "You know, when he left, I watched him from my bed. I could see where his car sat outside from there. Ma had followed him out after they'd been drinkin' on the porch together. I saw him shove her away. She kind of fell back...into the dirt."

"Did he look back?"

"Not once," Nick said. "She sat there for a while longer. I could hear her cryin'."

"You didn't go out to her?"

"Oh no," he said. "She didn't like me to know...ya know...when he disrespected her like that."

"Wasn't that all the time?"

Nick went on, distracted. "The next morning she never came out of her room. I thought I shoulda gone in to check on her, but I didn't. I mean, anything coulda happened after that and all I thought was, well, at least now maybe I'll get outta this shithole."

"Did you?"

"Hell no. I didn't get out 'til I moved out myself. She stopped tryin' to make things better. When she finally came out of that room, she'd become a lost soul. But,

Gracie, he didn't do that to her. Not all of it, anyway. She coulda left him. She deserved better than what she got, sure. But she shoulda left him."

Gracie reached over and patted Nick's back. "I think we all deserved better than what we got," she said.

She walked a few paces, gazing up at the treehouse where they'd played together as kids. "Remember that summer we were eight?" She knew he would. After all, he had broken his arm that summer, falling from high up as she had looked on, unable to grab onto his hand at the last moment.

"Yeah," he said, walking past her and putting his hand on the wooden ladder that was attached to the tree. "Spent that whole summer scared to climb up."

"Remember what finally made you do it?"

"It was that tornado siren goin' off. We were down the street at Grant's house. You'd kicked off your shoes when it started raining, and you got grass clippings all over your feet. You tore off when you heard that siren start, hollerin' back that you wanted to see it. I didn't even think about it, just ran after you."

"Mama came running outside, but I ran past her and climbed up. Pretty soon your mom came out yelling for you, too, but you followed me up without even thinking. When you made it to the top, I whipped around and yelled at you that you'd done it."

"But, they made us get down and go back inside to wait it out." Finn smiled, the memory coming to him as he spoke. "Your shoes sat outside of Grant's house for two weeks 'til you finally went and got them."

"Only because Mama said she wouldn't be buying me another pair of shoes again if I lost this one, too. Would've been the third pair that summer."

He was watching her. She could feel it with every part of her being. Was she so different now from that girl? She turned to him as he reached up, pulling himself to the top. "What are you waiting for?" he asked.

In that moment she felt like she had never been gone. How did he do that to her? Make her feel like no time had passed? A gust of wind came through and she felt the corners of her mouth turn up in a smile. Then, she started to climb.

11.

"YOU THINK WE'LL GET OUTTA HERE, FINN?" GRACIE ASKED, the sun beating down on her back as they sat on the edge of the water. She was wearing one of Hannah's bathing suits that she'd stolen from her room the night before, knowing she'd be heading to the beach today with her friends. Finn had just turned 18, the first of them to do so, being almost a year older than the rest of them. He'd wanted to spend the day outside, and in Glenwood that meant driving down to Rockdale to the beach.

A bird flew overhead, casting a shadow on them briefly. Finn slipped off his sunglasses after, as if the quick shadow had somehow alerted him of the sun's glaring light. "I sure hope so," he said, leaning back onto the sand.

While it was late August, the heat was less intense than it had been, and a soft breeze had kept them cool that afternoon.

"Mary Ellen got into a private college out west. Did you hear that? They offered her a full ride."

"Wish I were smart enough for that," Finn said.

"You are smart enough."

"Not Mary Ellen smart, not by a long shot. Can you imagine not havin' any student loans? Just movin' across the country and livin' for free?"

Gracie shook her head. No, she couldn't imagine it. That was someone else's life.

"Well, lookie here," they heard from behind them.

"Riley Walker, don't go sneakin' up on people. You about scared me outta my skin!" Gracie said when she turned and saw him standing there. He and two other boys from their class, Bill Deegan and Carter Parnell, were with him.

"That was the idea," he replied, laughing. "You guys just hangin' out? Where's Grant?"

Finn got up so he was standing with them. "Aw, Riley, you know he and Liv are off somewhere."

"Anywhere so they won't see the likes of you," Gracie added.

"C'mon Gracie. Lighten up. Besides, I thought you two might want to come to a party I'm havin' later tonight."

"Parents outta town?" Finn asked.

"For a whole week before the year starts again."

"If I was your Mama, I'd need a week off every once in a while, too," Gracie said, winking at Finn.

Riley shot her a look. "My mama loves me, thank you very much."

"You boys goin'?" Finn asked, looking to Bill and Carter.

"Plannin' to," Carter said.

"If all the ladies Riley says are comin' actually show, it'll be one hell of a party," Bill added.

"You can count on us," Finn said. Gracie rolled her eyes and laid back on her towel. Why Finn wanted to hang out with these guys was beyond her. She'd never been part of Finn's crowd, at least not the way other girls were. Most of them didn't understand why he even bothered with her. He, Grant and Olivia had all transitioned to high school with no issues, but she wasn't so lucky. She couldn't figure out the unspoken code of conduct among the popular kids, or maybe she just didn't care.

"Alright. Nine o'clock. Let Grant and Liv know. See you then." Riley gave them both a wave, turning back to his buddies and moving on down the beach to share the party news with other classmates there.

"See you," Finn said, sitting back down.

The sun had started to lower in the sky, and Gracie's stomach growled. She looked at her phone, checking the time. "Close to dinner. Mama'll be wanting me home soon."

"Yeah, think she'll let you out tonight?"

"She's workin' a lot lately," Gracie said.

"If you don't want to go, we don't have to."

"No, it's alright. I'll go."

Finn looked at her, putting a hand on her knee. "I mean it, Gracie. I don't care about Riley's party. If you don't want to go, we can do somethin' else."

She'd much rather just hang out with Grant and Liv. The four of them always managed to find things to do. Finn looked at her, expectantly. "It's fine," she said, finally. And then, sounding much less sure. "We should go."

"Yeah?"

"Yeah."

"You've never liked Riley much, have you?"

Gracie sighed. "He's just obnoxious, Finn. I know he's your friend, but I just don't get it."

"Aw, he's harmless."

"Maybe I'm just being difficult," she said, finally. "I've never really fit in with you guys."

"You're too hard on yourself, you know. People just want to have a good time. You can be a bit serious for them, I think."

"I can have fun, too."

"Oh, really?" He looked doubtful.

"Finn Miller, tonight I'll show you just how much fun I can have."

He looked up, a twinkle in his eye. "I can't wait."

"Holy shit," Grant said as they pulled up to Riley's house.

"Holy shit is right," Olivia agreed.

Gracie guessed their whole school was at the party, and maybe even a few other schools in the state. She'd never seen so many people on one lawn.

"Good thing Riley lives so far out," Finn added.

They'd come in Grant's truck, Finn and Gracie sitting in the bed. He parked and they got out, just as Carter and Sadie, another girl from their class, passed by.

"Hey man, you made it," Carter said, seeing Finn and giving him a high-five. "Beer's over there." He pointed toward the backyard.

"Thanks," Finn said. "Riley invite the whole county?"

"Looks like it, don't it?"

"He's gonna have some people sleepin' on his lawn tonight I reckon," Sadie offered as Carter put an arm around her.

Gracie adjusted the necklace she was wearing. "Where'd you say the beer was?" she asked. Finn's eyebrow went up, and she brushed her bangs out of her eyes.

"Other side of the garage," Sadie said.

The four of them made their way to the back, Olivia stopping to chat with some girls on her cheerleading squad. Finn filled a cup from the keg and passed it to her. He knew she rarely touched the stuff, staying away from parties she'd never been fully comfortable at. "Now, don't go and get too crazy."

"Don't you worry about me," she said, gulping down some of the beer.

"Gracie Brannen, you drinkin' tonight?" Grant asked, his eyes wide. "Well, I'll be. This is gonna be a helluva party after all."

"Guess that makes me the DD," Olivia said, catching up to them.

"If you don't mind," Grant said, putting an arm around her.

"Nah, I've got to get up early tomorrow," she said. "Cheer camp."

"Hey, Finn," they all turned, seeing Riley on the front porch. "Get in here!"

Grant rolled his eyes. He was all too familiar with Riley's rowdy ways.

"Be right back," Finn said.

Gracie waved him off. "Don't worry about me. I'll be livin' it up by the time you get back."

"Right," he said before turning to go. She watched them walk up to the house, their silhouettes growing smaller in the distance.

"Gracie, I need to go talk to Beth real quick. We're riding to camp together tomorrow. Will you be alright?"

"Aw, Liv, I don't need a babysitter."

She patted Gracie on the shoulder. "I just want to make sure you won't run off as soon as I'm gone. I know you just love these parties."

"I promise I'll be right here where you left me," she said, taking another big sip from her cup. The beer was going down much easier than she thought it would, and it made her feel a little less self-conscious in this unfamiliar environment.

Her answer must have been acceptable. Olivia bounded off to find Beth as Gracie finished off her beer. She turned to refill it, then walked along the fence line, looking for a familiar face. She saw kids from school, but they seemed different here. They were living on adrenaline and teenage idealism, shouting to each other across the yard, desperate for attention and terrified of being left out.

"You friends with Riley?" she heard a voice behind her ask.

Turning, she saw him leaning against the fence. "Who's asking?" She took another drink from her cup, letting the alcohol dull her senses.

"Brooks Talhoun," he said, turning his body toward her, his arm still resting on the top of the wood fence. "Riley's older and much less annoying cousin."

She took a step toward him. "Gracie Brannen," she said. He was attractive, more so than Riley, at least, though he had curly hair that was a bit too long for Gracie's taste, and she could barely see his eyes from underneath it.

"Nice to meet you, Gracie Brannen."

She felt herself blush, then took another sip from her cup. It surprised her, considering all she'd felt for Brooks' cousin was utter repulsion. "You go to school around here?" she asked.

"Nope, I live in Tennessee. Came for a visit and to watch over Riley."

She felt herself laugh before she heard it. "You're not doin' a very good job, are you?"

"Oh, you mean this?" He motioned to the crowd of people in front of them. "This is nothing."

"I'm sure Riley's parents wouldn't say it was nothing," she said.

He didn't respond, and she wondered if she was being a killjoy. She was fooling herself thinking she could be at ease in this type of situation. She leaned back, raising her cup, and drank the rest of it down.

"So, Gracie Brannen," he said. "You in Riley's class?"

"I am."

He reached into his pocket and pulled out a flask. "Seventeen?" he asked.

Gracie nodded. She couldn't tell how old he was.

He turned the cap on the flask, then held it out for her. "Whiskey?"

She looked around, searching the yard for Finn. When she turned her attention back, he was still holding out the flask. What the hell, she thought. She took a swig, coughing after. Brooks laughed, so she took another.

"Not much of a drinker, are you?" he asked, taking the flask back.

She shrugged. No sense in pretending.

"You seem older than seventeen," he said. He was studying her in the way that Finn did, and it made her uncomfortable. She'd never had another boy's attention before.

"I'll be eighteen in a few months."

He laughed again. Was she being funny?

"I just mean you don't seem to fit in with these other kids. You stand out."

"Is that bad?" she asked.

"Not at all."

They were quiet a moment, standing together. Gracie saw Finn come out of the house, searching the yard for her. "I better go," she said.

"Sure, Gracie Brannen," he said, still watching her. Why did he keep saying her whole name?

"Thanks for the drink," she said, pointing to the flask. She turned and walked across the yard.

"Who was that?" Finn asked when she approached him.

"Riley's cousin, I guess."

"What'd he want?"

Gracie shoved Finn in the shoulder. "Finn Miller, wipe that look off your face this minute. You don't own me. I can talk to whoever I please."

Finn narrowed his eyes at her, and she felt dizzy. "Maybe this was a bad idea," he said. She looked back the way she'd just come. Brooks was still there, watching them.

"Oh, I'm havin' a fine time. Just relax."

"Gracie, I took it upon myself to get you another," Grant said, offering her a full cup.

"Why thank you," Gracie said, taking it from him.

"Actually, I think it's time to go," Finn said.

"What?" Grant wasn't much for leaving parties, and Olivia wouldn't want to go when they'd just gotten there. "Have you turned into Gracie now that she's finally having fun?"

Finn didn't say anything, but looked back in Brooks' direction.

"He's just fine," Gracie said. "In fact he's so fine, he wants to get in on that game of flippy cup," she said, pointing to the other end of the lot.

Grant didn't wait for Finn to respond. He grabbed his shoulder and pushed him in the direction of the game. "We'll be back, Gracie." She gave a little wave as they disappeared into the crowd, then turned and walked toward the house, looking for Olivia, instead running into Poppy. Poppy was in her English class, and sat right in front of her. Her hair, which was a mass of dark brown curls, always blocked her view.

"Gracie, who were you talkin' to earlier?" she asked, her voice high and shrill.

She looked over her shoulder. "Who? Him?"

"Yes," Poppy said, her eyes bulging.

"That's Riley's cousin."

"Do you know him somehow?"

She shook her head. "I only just met him."

Poppy looked disappointed.

"Do you think you could introduce us?" she asked, sheepishly.

Gracie contemplated this. Poppy Goldman was one of the popular kids—one of the girls Gracie knew looked down on her. Is this what parties and drinking did to people? Put them all on an equal playing field, forgetting who was who and all the bullshit rules of high school?

"Sure," she said, finally, taking Poppy's hand. They weaved through the crowd, stopping in front of Brooks. Gracie felt invincible, and she liked the feeling. She wondered if her daddy felt the same every time he had a drink. It made her feel guilty. "Brooks, this is my friend, Poppy." She turned to Poppy who was bright red and smiling like a lovesick schoolgirl. "Poppy, this is Riley's cousin, Brooks."

"Nice to meet you, Poppy," Brooks said, not taking his eyes off Gracie.

"You live around here?" Poppy asked. Gracie turned, suddenly feeling like she needed to sit down. She headed for the barn, hearing Poppy yapping behind her. When she got there, she went inside and leaned against the wall. She felt warm and sick, and she smelled like home.

"You okay?" she heard behind her.

She looked up. "I'll be fine."

"Shouldn't have given you that whiskey."

He leaned his back onto the wall, bending down to meet her eyes. She raised her head up and rubbed her eyes.

"So, is that guy you were talking with earlier your boyfriend?" he asked.

She nodded.

"Too bad," he said. She felt too bad to be flattered.

She mustered up a smile. "I've known him since I was born."

Brooks crossed his arms. "You gonna marry him?"

What kind of question was that? "I suppose. Someday."

"And you never wonder whether there's anyone else out there?"

"Like you, you mean?" she asked.

"Sure, like me. Like anyone. There are a lot of people in the world, you know."

Gracie didn't know what to say. All she'd ever thought about was getting out of Glenwood, and Finn had always been part of those plans.

Before she could think of a response, he was kissing her. Stunned, she pulled away.

"Don't settle down before you're ready," he said, then walked out of the barn. Gracie put a hand to her mouth, feeling dazed.

A few minutes later, Olivia appeared. "There you are!" Gracie looked up. "Finn wants to go. You ready?"

Gracie nodded, following Olivia out of the barn.

"What were you doin' in there by yourself anyway?"

"Oh, nothing." She looked back over her shoulder as they headed to the car. Brooks was standing along the fence, where she'd first seen him. When he saw her look back, he gave a little wave. She quickly turned back around, but she could still feel his lips on hers when she climbed into the truck where Finn sat waiting.

12.

THE SKY WAS OVERCAST WHEN FINN CAME TO HANNAH'S TO
pick her up. Gracie had been looking out the bedroom
window, searching the sky for any hint of rain, but so far
it had held off. When she saw him pull up, her eyes darted
around the room, finally falling on her jacket. Better to be
safe than sorry, she thought, tucking it under her arm.
Finn was already inside, kneeling down by Cayla when
she walked into the living room.

"Gracie," Cayla said when she saw her come in. "Can I
please go with you?"

Gracie smiled, happy to know that Cayla wanted to be
included, but shook her head. "Not this time, sweet pea,"
she said. The little girl frowned, but her unhappiness
didn't last long, as her curiosity got the best of her.

"Where are you going?" she asked, turning her
attention back to Finn.

"We're just going into Ashland for a while."

"But I love it there." The girl was not going to give up.

Hannah flew into the room, her mother's intuition
right on the nose. "Not today, Cayla. And besides, they're
going to do boring old grown-up stuff. You and I are
going to decorate cupcakes."

Cayla's eyes sparkled. "Cupcakes?"

"Mm-hmm."

"With sprinkles?"

"With sprinkles."

Cayla bounded out of the room faster than a jackrabbit on steroids.

"You two have fun," Hannah said, retreating just as quickly.

Gracie watched her go then turned to Finn. "Hi," she said, smiling.

"Hi," he said, smiling back.

"So, where are we off to?"

He opened the door, holding it open for her and they made their way to his car. It was a black Jeep Grand Cherokee, sleek and sturdy, a car built for the likes of Finn Miller. "Well, I thought we'd stop by my place. I've got to pick up a few things and drop them at the office. After that, I thought dinner. Maybe a walk down by the promenade."

"Sounds good to me." Gracie slid into the passenger seat, buckling herself in. Although the car was much nicer than what he'd driven back in high school, there was a feeling of déjà vu as she settled into the seat. She looked over at Finn to see if he felt it, too, but he didn't seem to notice.

The drive to Ashland was quick. There were newly-built houses along the route they took, where Gracie was fairly certain she remembered it used to be farmland. She thought she recognized a few of the older buildings here and there, but everything looked so different that she couldn't be sure. When they pulled into town, Gracie was pleasantly surprised. What once had been a shabby, rundown city with no particular attractive qualities was now a bustling city center. Finn pointed out areas of town, talking about the bars, restaurants and shops that now stood where open lots and vacant buildings once polluted the streets. Gracie couldn't believe her eyes. As a child, she remembered looking out the window as they drove around the city, thinking she wouldn't get out of the car if her mother promised her heaps of candy in return. Now, she looked in awe at the storefronts and diners enjoying their meals on restaurant patios, and she wondered how a city could change that quickly. Or maybe she wasn't remembering it quite right.

"Looks a bit different from when we were kids, doesn't it?" Finn asked, breaking the silence.

"I hardly recognize it." Gracie rolled the window down, letting the sights and sounds fill the car.

They came to a stoplight and Finn flipped on his signal. "My place is just around the corner," he said pointing. They approached a brick building with the numbers 777, in white, along the side. Finn pulled up to a parking meter out front and turned off the car. "No parking?" Gracie asked.

"It's around back," he said, taking the keys out of the ignition. "We won't stay long."

Gracie got out of the car and looked around. The building was prime real estate, across from a huge green space where groups of people were dispersed intermittently about. On either side of the building were upscale eateries, one Italian, the other sushi. Finn dug in his pocket for a few quarters, then slipped them into the meter, turning to Gracie after he'd done so. "Ready?"

She followed him to the elevator inside and they took it up to the fifth floor. When they got off, they walked down a long hall to the very last door.

"This is me. Now, don't judge. Remember, I'm a bachelor."

He opened the door, and they walked inside. Gracie had expected an unkempt space, lacking artistry and design. Finn's home was anything but that. The loft-style apartment featured an exposed brick wall on one side, concrete floors, granite countertops and beautiful artwork throughout. She saw a piece featuring a jazz player and another much larger piece done in black and white tones, with a girl's face at the center, in blue. The artwork was vibrant and Gracie found herself immediately taken in by the colors in each piece, as they were in such contrast to the dark hues of the wood, walls and furniture in the place. "I'm not sure what you meant by 'don't judge,' Finn, but this place is amazing." He was obviously doing well for himself. She couldn't guess what a place like this might cost, but it had to be a lot.

Finn shrugged. "Thanks." He put his keys on the table near the door, then walked past Gracie. "Make yourself at home. I just need to grab those papers quick." He walked to the stairs leading up to the lofted bedroom and walked up, disappearing for a moment.

Gracie moved toward the living room and the huge window in front of her. When she looked out, she saw a couple walking a Great Dane in the grassy area across the street. "That's Muir Park," Finn said, startling her. She jumped back and almost ran into him, catching herself on the sofa beside her.

"This is quite a place, Finn. I'm happy to know you're doing so well for yourself."

"Thank you," he said, his eyes moving down below to where she had been looking a moment before. "Can I get you something to drink? How about a martini?"

"Uh, sure." She was used to drinking beer and didn't have much of a taste for the fancier drinks, but she felt like maybe she needed to be fancy standing in Finn's sophisticated apartment.

He went over to the kitchen. She sat down on the couch, trying not to feel so out of place.

"How long have you lived here?" she asked.

"Two years now," he said as he mixed up the drinks. "I used to live with Tucker in a shanty of a place across town, but when he and Eliza got engaged, they moved out to the 'burbs and I moved here."

"Eliza?"

"Yeah, they met at one of our gigs. She's a great girl. Loud and opinionated."

"The opposite of Tucker, then?"

Finn smiled. "Yeah, but they suit each other. And she's opinionated in a sweet, sociable way."

"Tucker's married." She breathed out the words, at the same time wondering why these things were so hard for her to believe. People got married all the time.

"Yep, almost a year now."

Gracie felt her face grow warm as it always did when people talked about marriage. She rubbed her hands together, trying to shake off the uncomfortable feeling. "What about you, Finn? You seeing anybody?"

She turned her attention to him, wanting to see his reaction, but his body was facing away from her. He picked up their drinks and walked in, setting one on the coffee table in front of her. After he'd placed it there, his eyes met hers. "I'm not seeing anyone at the moment."

"I'm surprised," she said.

Finn sat down across from her, leaning back into the cream-colored leather chair. He looked amused. "You are?"

"You're doing pretty well for yourself," Gracie said, suddenly feeling bold in her new surroundings. "Surely the ladies are lining up."

"I'm not lacking in that department, no," he said. Was he goading her? This whole situation was entirely confusing.

"Why am I here, Finn?"

If he was startled by the question he didn't show it. "I wanted you to get a glimpse into my life. See where I live, maybe understand who I am now."

She wasn't sure if she believed him. "That's all?"

Their eyes met in a strange sort of stand-off. "Why do you think you're here, Gracie?" he asked.

"I'm not sure."

"You're never sure, are you?"

Gracie cleared her throat, a nervous habit when she didn't know what more to say. "Maybe this was a bad idea."

"What exactly is a bad idea?"

"Us. Hanging out together."

Finn hung his head, then reached for his glass and took a drink. When he stood up, his expression had changed. It wasn't angry, but there was something behind his eyes that told her to tread carefully. "What about you, Gracie? Are you seeing anybody back home?"

Home. It was funny thinking of it that way. She'd never thought of Pomroy as home.

"I was, but I'm not now."

"A serious relationship, then?" he asked, his voice soft. She wondered if he wanted to know the answer.

"As serious as it could be, I suppose."

"How long were you seeing each other, if you don't mind me asking?"

She took a sip of her drink. "I don't mind. I'd say about a year."

"What happened?" he asked.

"What always happens. He wanted me to commit, and I couldn't."

His shoulders relaxed at that. "Well, it looks like we still have something in common, after all."

"Is that why I don't see any trace of a woman in this apartment?" she asked.

"That and I work a lot."

She felt the urge to break through the tension in the room. "And you take on babysitting duties for Olivia and Grant."

"Yes, I take a break from my workaholic ways when I get 'the call' from Olivia."

"The call?"

"You know, the I'm-seconds-away-from-losing-my-mind-if-I-don't-have-a-break-from-these-kids call."

Gracie laughed. "I'd like to hear what that call sounds like." She finished off her drink, taking a deep breath after swallowing it down.

"Want another?" Finn asked.

"No, that's alright."

"Didn't like it?"

She'd liked it fine, but she guessed it was an acquired taste. "It was fine. I finished it, didn't I?"

"Yeah, but I remember that look. It's just the same as the one you gave Olivia when she wanted everyone to try sushi for her 16th birthday."

"No, it's not!" Gracie didn't remember giving a look, but she did remember the sushi. "And for your information, I do like sushi now."

"You do?"

She felt compelled to defend herself. "Yes, I'm not the hillbilly I once was, Finn."

"No one ever thought that, Gracie," he said before gulping down the last of his own drink.

Gracie stood up and began moseying around the place.

"I'd give you a tour, but what you see is pretty much it." He stood, picking up their empty glasses and taking them to the kitchen.

She followed him there and hopped onto one of the bar stools. "How far away is your office?"

"Just a few blocks. We can walk there. I'll just run in and hand these off," he said, picking up the papers he'd brought down.

"And then where will we be going?"

He smiled, wickedly. "For sushi, of course."

When they'd made their way to the restaurant, they were seated right away. Blue was a sophisticated place. The walls were a darker hue of the color, making it feel a lot more intimate than it might have otherwise.

"Are you hungry?"

"Starving."

The waitress took their drink orders. Gracie went with a Heineken. Finn ordered the same. "You know most girls order the girly drinks or wine on a date. But, you're not most girls, are you Gracie?"

"Is this a date?" she asked.

"It looks like one to me."

Shit.

She looked down at the menu. "What do you like?" she asked, changing the subject.

"Spicy tuna and the California roll."

"Well that's not too adventurous. I figured you'd be ordering something with squid or octopus."

"I've tried it," he said, his eyes moving from the menu to Gracie. "But I know what I like."

She felt her cheeks turn red, yet again, which was beginning to become an unwelcome habit of hers around him. "I think I'll get the smoked salmon," she said.

The waitress came back for their orders and was off again a few seconds later when Gracie heard a voice from behind.

"Finn Miller!" She turned to see a pretty blonde girl walking toward them. "I saw you walk in, and couldn't leave before saying hello." She looked at Gracie, then smiled politely.

"Becca," Finn said. "This is my friend, Gracie. Gracie, this is Becca."

"It's nice to meet you," Becca said, before focusing again on Finn.

"A bunch of us were out the other night, and I thought to text you. We were just over on 30th, at O'Cleary's."

"Jason out with you, too?"

"Yeah, but he's been seeing someone new, so he flakes out pretty early these days."

"Yeah, that girl Rachel he met at that marketing summit."

Becca tossed her glossy hair back over her shoulder. Gracie fidgeted in her chair.

"Well, we'll probably be out this weekend if you're interested." She glanced at Gracie when she said it, then quickly diverted her eyes back to Finn. "Text me later." Then she was off, joining the group of people waiting to leave at the door.

Gracie picked up her bottle and took a big swig. Could this evening get any more awkward? She wondered how many girls in this city had found their way into Finn's life —or bed, for that matter.

"Becca's also a realtor in Ashland," Finn said after she'd gone. "She's with another company, but we see each other at different workshops and such." Gracie's head was spinning and she hated herself for feeling jealous. She felt like a hormonal teenager.

"She seems nice," she said. She was afraid to say anything else.

Thankfully, their waitress chose that moment to bring their food. They ate in silence, the run-in with Becca weighing on Gracie's mind. She felt so out of her element here. Finn's success seemed to outshine everything. His life had come together, just like Gracie had known it would—known it should. They'd both escaped the small-town life, and yet instead of feeling closer to Finn because of it, she felt further away, disjointed and removed.

A short while later, they found themselves walking along the streets of Finn's neighborhood.

"You like it here?" Gracie asked after they'd walked a few blocks.

Finn shrugged. "Sometimes I feel I could be anywhere. There are big cities in every state, ya know? And houses for sale everywhere. I could do what I do wherever I chose to live."

"That doesn't sound like a yes or no."

He stopped walking, and Gracie slowed to a stop once she realized it. The trees around them had come to life as a light breeze came through. Gracie's hair went wild, and she reached to push it from in front of her face. "This place is fine," he said, looking at the ground, his hands resting on his hips. "I'm not gonna lie, Gracie. I ended up here, in part, because I didn't know where else to go after school. I pushed myself so hard those first years out, but I still wanted to be near my friends and family, too. This just seemed to be the place I could do that. It's not far from Glenwood. It's growing. Has a lot to offer. I'm happy I'm here, but do I have to be? Not at all."

"I'm proud of you, Finn."

"Yeah?" They started to walk again.

"You did everything you set out to do," she said.

"And you didn't?"

"I didn't say that." She tugged at her cross-body bag, wishing she hadn't brought the stupid thing along. Usually, she tucked her ID and credit card into her pocket so she wouldn't have to carry anything so bulky. "I guess it's just taken me longer to get there."

He didn't respond, and they walked on, each deep in their own thoughts. The sun was going down, and the streetlights had turned on. They walked by a set of row houses, so uniform in design that it was hard to tell where one ended and another began.

"Let's head back," Finn said. "I have this funny feeling it might rain."

"Still a country boy at heart," Gracie said, smiling. He laughed.

They made their way back, walking quickly and rounded the corner back to Finn's place. Gracie looked up to the sky as he found his keys. As they headed up to the apartment building, a few drops fell from the sky. Gracie shook her head in disbelief. Finn anticipated her reaction and held up his phone.

"Just got the weather alert."

Gracie rolled her eyes. "And I thought it was intuition."

As they made their way into the apartment, a steady rain began to come down outside. It wasn't the type that would last long, just a typical summer storm, over as quickly as it began.

"I've got to ask you one thing," Finn asked, tentatively, as Gracie took a seat on the couch.

"Okay."

"Did you know you were going to leave? When you came over that night?"

Gracie shook her head. "I didn't. Not right away, anyway."

"So, it was because of something I did or something I said."

She wasn't sure how to answer. "Not exactly."

"What does that mean?" he asked, his voice rising along with the emotion in his voice. He wasn't mad, but Gracie knew it wouldn't take long for him to get fed up.

"It just means that I realized we weren't on the same path."

"But you didn't feel the need to talk it over with me?"

"I knew you wouldn't let me go. You'd want to know why. You'd want to know what had changed."

He let out a deep breath, almost as if he was trying to calm himself and it took him a moment to speak again. "Of course I'd want to know. Like I said, I had loved you my entire life, Gracie. I thought you felt the same."

Finn moved to the couch, sitting down beside her.

"It happened a long time ago, and we're different people now. Can't we just let it be?"

He shook his head, a slow movement back and forth. "I don't think we're *that* different, are we?" His head was only inches away from hers, and she thought for a minute that he might lean in and kiss her, but he didn't. He leaned back into the couch, putting his hands behind his head. "We always end up in the same spot when we have this conversation. I don't want to do that tonight. I'll drop it for now."

She was grateful. She wanted to spend just one night with him where they didn't end up fighting about the past.

"So, tell me more about your job," he said. "What do you love most about it?"

She smiled and leaned back on the couch next to him, relaxed now. "I think I was made for it. I love being around the kids. Seeing them go from sick to well so quickly is extremely satisfying. And I like seeing that whole family dynamic. When a child is the patient, you really get to know entire families."

"Is it hard to say goodbye to them once they leave?"

She nodded. "Sometimes. If they're leaving, though, usually it's because they're better. If I'm feeling anything but happy about that, it's a little selfish."

"I bet you're a good nurse," he said, patting her on the knee. She wasn't ready for the wave of electricity she felt shoot through her body at his touch. She tried not to think about it.

"I try to be," she said. "It's my life, you know? I'm happiest when I'm there."

"You don't like being home?" There was that word again. Home.

"It's fine, I guess." She couldn't think of one reason why she liked to be at her apartment. It was small, dingy and lonely. "What about you?"

"Eh. It's somewhere to rest my head."

"Well, your somewhere looks pretty good to me. My place doesn't even come close to this."

"That bad, huh?"

"It's pretty bad," she said, looking around the room. "Imagine the exact opposite of this place. That's my place."

He laughed as Gracie's phone beeped. She dug into her bag and fished it out. *On your way back?* it read. She turned to Finn. "Hannah. I'm sure her mothering instincts are kicking in."

Finn pulled his phone out, looking at the time. "Already eleven. Where did the time go?" He set his phone on the coffee table. "Should we go?"

She nodded, and they got up to leave. But she couldn't help but wonder, as they walked to the car, what would happen if she stayed.

13.

THE STRAWBERRIES LOOKED GOOD. GRACIE ALWAYS HATED IT when she bought a carton at the supermarket and the next day they were turning brown. It felt like she'd been punked by the grocers. She inspected the carton, looking at each berry, and she could almost taste the juices right then.

She'd come to get the ingredients for the marshmallow pizza she had promised Cayla, but drifted to the produce department, wondering if Cayla would mind if she bought an angel food cake instead. These strawberries would be the perfect complement, along with some honey drizzled on top. She guessed Cayla would most definitely mind since she'd talked about the marshmallow pizza every day since Gracie had mentioned.

"Gracie Brannen, is that you?" she heard behind her.

She turned, placing the strawberries in her basket. "Poppy?" she asked, immediately recognizing the woman.

"Well, I'll be. I haven't seen you since high school!"

Not wanting to state the obvious, that she hadn't been back since then, her reply mimicked Poppy's astonished tone. "Has it been that long?"

"I reckon so," Poppy answered, pushing her cart to where Gracie was standing. Her smile quickly vanished, quickly changing to a look of sympathy. "I heard the news about your mama. Such a shame."

It didn't surprise Gracie. This town was so small, news traveled as fast as a pup with his tail on fire.

"Thank you," Gracie said, picking up another carton of strawberries. How long would she have to make small talk, she wondered. Poppy had never been very interested in her life before.

"So, where do you live now?" she asked, leaning against the cart so it was holding her up, balancing her. Poppy had put on some weight since school. Gracie wondered if she had a litter of kids at home.

"Oh, I'm a nurse in Pomroy."

"A nurse?" Poppy looked impressed. "That's a lot of hard work, day in, day out. My sister's a nurse up in Kansas. Works her butt off, I tell ya."

Gracie smiled politely. "I work at a children's hospital, nights mostly." She felt the urge to take the focus off of herself. "What about you?"

"Oh, nothin' as fancy as that. I've been helpin' Randall out on the farm, and I work a few shifts at Darla's Fashions on the weekends."

Randall Granger was a year ahead of them in school. Gracie never would have pictured the two of them together back then, but she guessed when only a handful of kids stayed on in Glenwood, while the rest went out to search for something beyond, there were only so many options.

"We've got four little rugrats runnin' around, too."

"Well, that'll keep you busy." She looked past Poppy to the display of bananas behind her, trying to send a hint that she needed to return to her shopping. Poppy was oblivious.

"So, you seen Finn lately? I was drivin' down 245 and wouldn't you know, I saw his face on a giant billboard!"

For God's sake, she couldn't talk to anyone in this town without hearing Finn Miller's name. "I've seen him," she replied. "Haven't seen the billboard, though."

Poppy put her hand in the air, her eyes rolling back as she gasped loudly. Had she always been so dramatic? "Well, you can't miss it! He's still as handsome as ever, too." She winked at Gracie. "I'll tell you everyone got the shock of their life hearin' the two of you broke things off."

This was not a conversation Gracie wanted to have in the middle of a supermarket, and Poppy Goldman—or Granger, it probably was now—was definitely the last person she would ever want to have it with. She needed to get out of here. "I'm sure people had better things to do than worry about the state of Finn and I's relationship," she said. Poppy straightened up, surprised at Gracie's aloofness. She must have thought Gracie was just waiting to spill her heart out to someone. Like an old high school acquaintance. Like maybe Poppy Goldman. Gracie didn't give her time to think on it. "Well, I've got to pick up a few more things. Nice runnin' into you, Poppy." She gave a little wave, and preceded down the aisle, leaving Poppy to take what she wanted from her response. Gracie guessed she'd be on her phone within minutes, telling whatever Glenwood classmates she kept in touch with that she'd just seen Gracie Brannen back in town, and that she was definitely an uppity snob, as they surmised everyone who left town, only to come back infrequently for visits turned out to be.

She walked through the aisles until she finally found the one with the marshmallows. She gathered up a few bags of the colored ones, thinking it'd be more fun for Cayla to have a pink, yellow and green marshmallow treat than plain old white. She found the chocolate chips, and as she went by the cake decorating items, she grabbed some sprinkles, too, because if you're going to have marshmallow pizza, you might as well go all out. With that, she walked to the freezer section and picked up some refrigerated pizza dough. After being stopped by Poppy, she'd forgotten to grab the angel food cake she'd craved, so she walked back to the front of the store to the bakery.

Her one and only true interaction with Poppy had been at Riley Walker's party, and she barely remembered that. She tried not to think of that party, it being the source of her and Finn's only fight, him green with jealousy and drunk from too many rounds of flippy cup. In fact, she'd almost forgotten about it, and her short interaction with Brooks Talhoun.

Grabbing the cake, she moved to the only open register, placing her items on the belt before swiping her credit card through the reader. The cashier, a slim woman with a toothy grin, smiled at her as she picked up her bags. As she turned to leave, she spotted Poppy from behind the cart corral.

She ducked down and made a bee-line for the exit.

Cayla poured the chocolate chips onto the pizza dough. "Can I have one, Aunt Gracie?" she asked, already picking one out of the pile.

"Just one," Gracie said, trying to think what Hannah would say if she let her eat them all up. "We need them for the pizza."

"Oh, alright." The little girl continued to stare longingly at the chocolates.

"Okay, time for the marshmallows!" Cayla poured the bag out while Gracie spread them out over the chocolate chips.

"Now the sprinkles?" Cayla asked, picking up the container of rainbow sprinkles.

"Not yet. Those are for after it's cooked."

Gracie reached up, picking Cayla up off the counter and placing her back on the ground. Backing up, she opened the oven as Cayla watched, putting the tray in to cook.

"How long will it take?" Cayla asked, kneeling down and looking into the window as the pizza began to cook.

"Just about 20 minutes."

"Twenty minutes!" Cayla exclaimed. A lifetime to a six-year-old chocolate fiend.

"Yep. Just enough time for you to eat your dinner."

Cayla made a face.

"You've got to eat dinner before dessert."

"But, it's pizza. Pizza *is* dinner."

The kid had a point. Gracie took the spaghetti that had been boiling off the stove and drained it. As she dished it up, Cayla made her way to the table.

"So, what do you think your mom and dad are doing tonight?" she asked.

Cayla shrugged.

"You gonna save them a piece of pizza?"

"No way! It's just for you and me, Aunt Gracie."

She couldn't help but laugh. She and Hannah had been the same way. She leaned over the stove, turning the knob that controlled the front burner to off. Her phone buzzed a minute later.

"Text message, Aunt Gracie!" Cayla yelled before inhaling a forkful of noodles, the sauce running down her chin.

"That's gonna drip right onto your pretty pink shirt," she said as she left the room to get her phone.

Heard you ran into Poppy today, it read. From Olivia. Dang, word got around quick here, she thought before punching in a response.

Not the best part of my day.

Well, it was hers!

Gracie couldn't help but laugh. Of course it was. The woman probably lived for new gossip.

"Aunt Gracie! I'm finished eating my spaghetti!"

"Be right there!"

She could smell the chocolate on the marshmallow pizza cooking, the aroma wafting to the living room and invading her nostrils.

I bet. Walk tomorrow?

A few seconds later her phone buzzed again. *7?*

7 it is. Meet you at your place.

She tucked the phone into her back pocket then re-entered the kitchen. "Cayla!" she exclaimed when she saw her niece. "What happened?"

"Nothing. I just ate my dinner like I was supposed to," she said.

"You're covered in sauce!"

Cayla giggled. "Mama makes me take my clothes off to eat spaghetti."

"I can see why. Aren't you a little old to make a mess like this?"

The little girl shrugged. "Spaghetti is hard to eat." Fair enough. How many times had she herself slopped sauce onto her shirt, and she was well past the age of six. Gracie helped her take her clothes off, checking the timer on the oven. Two minutes. She looked back to the counter where her own bowl of cold spaghetti sat waiting. She could heat it up, she supposed. Nah, she thought, tonight was definitely a marshmallow pizza kind of night.

"So that's it?" Olivia asked as they wound around the edge of the property. She and Grant owned seven acres that included a small pond at the very back. Olivia had suggested they walk to it, then decide if they wanted to go further, hiking into the brush behind it.

"That's it. I barely said anything to her," Gracie said. "How'd you even hear about it anyway?"

"Grant saw Randall over his lunch break. Said Poppy came home gabbin' on and on about it."

Gracie rolled her eyes. Some things never changed.

"I don't really want to talk about Poppy Granger," Olivia said, adjusting her sunglasses.

"Good, neither do I," Gracie agreed.

"I want to know about your date!"

"Oh, Liv," she sighed, wondering what to tell her friend, and how much of what she said would get back to Finn. "It was fine."

"Any old sparks?"

She didn't respond. "He's the same old Finn in some ways," she said. "Then again, he's different, too. He's got quite the setup in Ashland."

"He's worked hard for it."

"We ran into a girl he knew at the restaurant."

Olivia raised an eyebrow. "Oh yeah?"

"I think she thought I was invading her turf or something."

"She was interested in him, then?"

"I don't know. Maybe. She definitely gave me the once-over."

"Well, Finn's quite a catch, Gracie. You of all people know that."

She did know that, which is why it had been so difficult to say goodbye to him that night.

They approached the pond, each of them slowing down their pace as they drew closer. Gracie saw the water ripple where a fish must have jumped from the water, though she didn't see it. The air was humid and she wished she had a spray bottle to spray the back of her neck to cool it down. She reached down, cupping some of the pond water and lifting it to her shoulders, letting it splash onto her skin.

"Just don't drink it," Olivia warned. "You never know what's runnin' off from the fields."

Gracie nodded, remembering a time when they all swam in the ponds, not thinking of chemicals and cancer and all the bad things that could happen. Back when they could just live summer. Breathe it. That way of life seemed long gone.

"You still love him?" Olivia asked as they started walking again, rounding the pond.

"I don't know, Liv. It was such a long time ago..." Even as she said it, she knew it didn't matter. "It would never work."

"Have some faith, Gracie. Things always work out in the end."

"Do they?"

"I believe they do."

Gracie picked up her pace, striding out to keep up with Olivia, wishing it were that easy.

"Git me another beer, will you?" Gracie heard through her bedroom door. She opened it quietly, peeking around to see her daddy in the living room, watching TV. Her mother had gone into the kitchen and when she came out she plopped a bottle beside him, then turned to leave. "Where do you think you're off to, then?" he said, not letting her off the hook that easily.

"I've got some gardening to do," she said. "Why don't you take a nap, and I'll be in shortly to make dinner."

He scoffed, getting up from his chair. Gracie wondered why he couldn't have done that a few minutes ago and gotten his own beer. He sidled up to her mama, his eyes squinting so he could focus on her. "You tryin' to tell me what to do?"

"Now, Jack, you know I'm not. I'm just letting you know when dinner will be. I thought you looked tired, too, so suggested a nap."

His face contorted and Gracie thought for moment that he was just about the ugliest person she'd ever seen. Whatever her mother said was going in one ear and out the other. "Think you're better than me? You've always thought so. Don't try and hide it now."

Mama sighed, her arms hanging limp at her sides. "I don't think that. I've always loved you, the best I know how."

He didn't hear her. "You think I can't take care of this family? That I'm not man enough?"

"Of course not," she said, backing away from him. Gracie heard a noise behind her and saw Hannah appear in the doorway. She put a finger up to her mouth to shush her, then turned her attention back to the living room.

"I've done everything for you and those girls," he hissed. "It's never enough."

Her mother's back was rigid, and she watched him flail about in front of her as if she'd seen it a thousand times before, and she probably had. "I know how much you do."

"Ah, hell, you don't know nothin'. I've gotta take care of this family. If it was up to the likes of you, we'd be eatin' beans and potatoes every night."

"You're absolutely right," she said. Mama knew there was no arguing with him, so she let him say anything he wanted, no matter how much it hurt her. She kept calm and cool, but that just infuriated him further.

"You antagonizin' me?" He got right up in her face. Gracie couldn't stand it. She leapt from the doorway, Hannah right behind her.

"Don't talk to Mama like that," she yelled. It took a minute for her daddy to focus, and realize the voice had come from her. "She didn't do anything wrong, and she got you your stupid beer."

Mama shook her head at Gracie, trying to send her a signal to hush up.

"What did you say to me, girl?" He was on her in an instant, grabbing her neck and pushing her away from them. "Get on outta here. This is 'tween your mama and me." He let go of her and turned back to Mama.

"No, it ain't," Gracie said, crossing her arms in front of her.

"Gracie, stop," Hannah whispered from behind her. "Let's go out for a walk."

"No, H. He's got no right to treat us like this. Especially Mama, who does whatever he asks even when she shouldn't."

"Gracie Mae, please go with your sister," Mama said. "It's fine. Your daddy and I are just talkin' things over."

"You listen to your mama, now. Ya hear?" he said, his words slurring together.

"Mama, you don't have to let him treat you this way. He's not a good man." Gracie wasn't giving up. She couldn't stand to see her mother take one more condescending remark, or brush off one more of his criticizing comments.

"You see this?" her daddy yelled, turning to Mama. "This is from lettin' her gallivant around town doin' whatever she pleases. *With* whoever she pleases." His words were an accusation. "I told ya no good would come from lettin' her run around with that Miller boy. People are gonna think I can't control my own is what they'll think."

"What's that supposed to mean?" Gracie yelled back. She wasn't sure, but it sounded like her father was accusing her of something.

"People don't think nothin'" her mama said, quietly. "They're just kids, Jack."

"That don't make it right," he said.

Hannah had inched closer to them, and she moved her body so it was between their parents. Her older sister knew he wouldn't do anything to her, but if he got mad enough, he just might hit Mama. "Daddy, I'll go ahead and take Gracie down by the pond. We'll go fishin' then come back for supper and have a nice family meal."

"Thank you, Hannah," Mama said, a wave a relief showing across her face.

"Git on, then," Daddy said, patting Hannah on the shoulder. Even in the middle of a drunken tirade, he still found a way to love on his sweet Hannah. He smiled the only smile he could muster, then turned his attention back to Mama. "I swear if I didn't see you birth her with my own eyes, I wouldn't believe she was yours."

That was all it took. Gracie lunged at him, hitting his face with her small fists, barely making an impact. He tried to grab her, but he was too drunk, and kept missing her as she squirmed out of his reach.

"Gracie, stop!" Hannah yelled, her eyes full of fright. Mama reached for her, trying to pull her away.

"You're trash, Daddy." Her voice was hateful and mean. "Everybody says so. The whole town talks about you. How you cheat on Mama. Pass out drunk everywhere."

He was on the floor, and he looked up at her, his face contorted in rage. Mama had started crying, tears running down her cheeks. And Hannah was sadly shaking her head, knowing there was no turning back now that Gracie had brought it all out into the open. Daddy pulled himself up, then grabbed Gracie's arm and dragged her to the front of the house. Mama started screaming and she and

Hannah ran after them. He opened the front door and tossed her out onto the porch. She fell back, hitting her tailbone and cried out.

"You get on outta here before I do somethin' I can't take back," he said, then turned around. Hannah ran to her side, kneeling down beside her.

"C'mon, Gracie," she said, looping her arms under Gracie's. "You're gonna have to walk with me." She pulled her up and they started to make their way across the lawn. When Gracie looked back after they'd walked a few yards she saw her daddy shut the front door and she said a silent prayer, hoping that Mama was alright when they got back.

It had been five days since Mama's funeral. In that time, Gracie had managed to find her way back into Hannah's life, make amends with Olivia, form a bond with her young niece and yet, she hadn't been able to create any semblance of a relationship with Finn. It was likely impossible, too. Back when their friendship had first turned romantic, they had fallen into it easily. Gracie supposed it was probably harder when you tried it the other way around.

"What do you have planned for the day?" Hannah asked as she came into the kitchen. She took a glass from the cupboard and poured herself some orange juice.

"I think I might head to Ashland to the farmers' market. Olivia and Grant wanted to take the boys, and Finn was going to meet us there."

"Just like old times," Hannah said. She was leaning against the counter, holding a cup of coffee.

"Yeah," Gracie laughed. "Except now there are two kids to chase after."

"How are things between you guys?" Hannah asked. Gracie turned, then pulled out a chair and sat down at the table.

"Between me an' Finn?"

"Yeah."

Gracie shrugged. "I don't know."

"How is it being around him again?" Hannah wasn't going to give up that easy.

"Oh, H. It's not about that. It never was. I loved him then, and I probably love him still. But, to be together, I'd have to tell him what happened, and if I did, he'd never forgive me."

Hannah didn't say anything. She looked at the floor, tapping her fingers on her mug. After a while, she came to sit by Gracie at the table. "You've got to tell him, though, Gracie. You can't carry it around on your own forever."

"Why not?" she asked.

"Because she's his daughter, too."

"But she's gone, H. She's not coming back."

"I think he deserves to know the truth and grieve for her, too."

Gracie shook her head. "He'll hate me."

"You don't know that," she whispered. Reaching an arm around Gracie's shoulders, she pulled her sister close. "I know you want to protect him from hurting, but don't you think she deserves to have her memory live on in her father—as well as her mother?"

Gracie's eyes filled with tears.

Hannah was right. She'd known all along that Finn had to know. All this time, she'd carried Rosie with her. In every challenging situation she found herself asking "What would I tell Rosie to do?" It comforted her, finding small ways to be close to her when she'd never gotten an actual chance to know each other.

"You know, he never stopped loving you. I ran into him a few times over the years. He always asked about you."

"He's got a whole different life now. You should see his place! He's got his clients, his friends, he's even got actual paying gigs playing with his band. And I'm sure he's got endless options when it comes to the ladies."

"But you're home to him, Gracie. You two have always been that to each other. It doesn't matter how many years go by, how many conversations you don't have in between. When you see that person again, it's like no time has passed."

Gracie wiped under her eyes. She knew what Hannah was trying to say, but it still didn't change the events of the last few years. The things that had made them each into who they were now.

"Listen, you'll figure it out. Older sisters have a tendency to preach, and I don't want to do that. All I'm saying is he deserves to know. He deserves the chance to love Rosie, too."

Gracie's hand automatically went to her locket. Hearing Rosie's name made her heart drop to her stomach. Her name made everything that had happened feel real.

"I know. I'll tell him. I will."

Hannah reached up and pulled Gracie's head down, kissing her forehead.

"It will be okay," she said, looking into Gracie's eyes.

Gracie nodded, but she wasn't so sure. She knew Finn. He'd already made it clear that he hated that she'd left before talking to him, breaking them up with her absence. If he knew he'd had a daughter that he'd never known about? Gracie guessed hate wouldn't even begin to cover it.

14.

"HOW ABOUT THAT BOOTH? LOCALLY-MADE MAPLE SYRUP. Yum." Olivia pointed across the cordoned-off street they were standing on.

"Sounds like my kind of booth," Gracie said. She looked around, scouring the crowds on Center Street, where all of the booths were lined on both sides.

"Can we take some home with us?" Judd asked, his eyes wide with anticipation.

"Of course we can," she replied, taking his hand. The two young boys walked with them across the street and were the first to taste test the syrup when they got there. Grant and Finn had wandered off, looking for something to eat, leaving Olivia and Gracie to wrangle the boys on their own, which wasn't much of a task for Olivia, but was leaving Gracie anxious as they scampered around, having to be called back time and again.

"So," Olivia said, after putting some of the syrup on a tiny plastic spoon and tasting it. Her eyes closed briefly as she swallowed it up before she looked at the vendor and held up two fingers. She licked her lips then focused on Gracie. "How much longer are you planning to stay?"

Gracie contemplated this. "Actually, I've got to leave tomorrow."

If Olivia was surprised by this, Gracie couldn't tell. Olivia was taking a small bag filled with her two bottles of maple syrup from the vendor, who smiled appreciatively before turning to the next customer. "When will you be back?" she asked.

"Mama, look at us!" Judd yelled. He and Ezra were outside the maple syrup tent, dancing along to the music of the street musicians playing a few feet away.

"You two are the silliest boys I've ever seen," she said, walking out of the small shaded tent. Gracie followed, watching as Judd jumped up and down, and Ezra spun in circles as fast as he could.

"Probably in about a month, for Cayla's birthday party," she said.

Olivia was still watching her boys, but a smile crept onto her face. "Well, that's about the best thing you could've said," she said, finally turning to look at Gracie.

"You think you'll be able to keep from being sick of me? It's a long drive for sure, but I don't see why I can't make the trip every so often."

"Gracie Mae, we'll never get sick of seeing you." The boys were still dancing, and after a few moments Olivia's face had turned more solemn. "Can I ask you something? If it's too out of line, you don't have to answer."

"Sure."

"Well, it's just something I've been thinking about since the funeral. How you said you and your Mama had still been in touch." She paused, looking down at her shoes. "Were you in touch with Hannah, too?"

"I was at first, but it had tapered off these past few years."

"Did they know where you were?"

Gracie shook her head. "No one knew that, Olivia."

"Did they ask?"

"They did. Every time. I just couldn't tell them."

Olivia closed her eyes, disappearing into her own thoughts. "Liv? Is there something else you want to ask me?"

She opened them and crossed her arms in front of her. "I guess, I don't know. I guess I'm wondering if you ever thought about callin' me."

The band ended a song, and immediately started another one, causing the boys to hoot and holler with glee. Gracie wasn't sure what to say. "Truth be told," she said. "I didn't have the guts to call anyone. And I was too heartbroken to realize I should."

Nodding, Olivia took her hand and squeezed it. "I hope someday you'll tell me what happened." She moved her gaze back to Ezra, Judd and the other kids dancing along to the music, but she kept hold of Gracie's hand, and Gracie stood by her friend, not ready yet herself to let go.

"Breakfast burritos!" Grant said, handing them out to everyone.

"We already had breakfast today!" Judd asked.

"You said you were hungry, didn't you?" Grant asked. "But I can take it back..."

"No, no, no!" Judd said. "I'll eat it!"

"These smell amazing," Gracie said, unwrapping it and taking a bite in one swift movement.

"Delicious," Olivia said, chomping down on hers. They had found a small space to sit down about a block away from the market. The boys were wrestling and rolling around in the grass beside them, or had been before Grant handed them each a burrito.

"So what do you guys have planned for the rest of the day?" Finn asked Grant, wiping his mouth with the side of his hand. He was holding his burrito with the same one, and some scrambled eggs slipped out and fell onto the grass beside him. He batted it away with his free hand, breaking it apart and sending it flying.

"Ezra's got a baseball game later," Olivia said, looking up to the sky. "And it's going to be a hot one today."

Ezra looked up from his burrito. "The heat is nothin' to me," he said to Finn, who chuckled out loud.

Olivia rolled her eyes. "The boy would play baseball in subzero temperatures, too, if we let him. He's crazy about it. Me? Not so much." She leaned back on the tree behind her that was providing enough shade to make their morning outing tolerable.

"Liv's never been much for baseball," Grant said, gripping her shoulder with his bear-like hands and squeezing it, causing Olivia to rock back and forth with the motion.

"That may be true, hun, but I've never missed a game, have I?"

"That's true," he agreed.

"If I remember right, you never missed one of Grant's back in the day either," Finn said. Watching the three of them, Gracie could see the closeness. The way they interacted, spoke. It was like an endless conversation that never came to an end. They flowed along so easily, so casually, that it left Gracie feeling stimulated. She liked the feeling of being part of such closeness. A closeness, she realized, she greatly missed.

"Yeah, yeah," Grant said. "You're right. My girl, here, never missed a game of mine, either." He took a drink from his lemonade, then turned his attention to Olivia. "Well, I think you did miss one. What was it, the flu, right? Only person I know who gets the flu in the summer."

Olivia shook her head. "Don't remind me! I've never been so sick. Knock on wood." She hit the tree behind her with her fist.

"Yeah, I remember that," Gracie said. "We were supposed to go together."

"We were. I'd finally talked you into coming with me, and then I went and got the flu." Olivia's eyes narrowed and she shielded them from the sun with her hand. "Boys! Get back over here this minute!" Gracie followed her gaze to see Ezra and Judd running off in the other direction. When they heard their mom's voice, they hightailed it back, collapsing next to Finn. "Finn," Judd said, the top of his head shimmering with sweat. "Do you think we're old enough to go around by ourselves?"

"Not without permission," Finn said. He winked at Olivia, and she stifled a smile.

"You never did?"

"Never."

"Aw, I don't believe you." The boy laid his head back in the grass, putting his arm over his face, hiding it.

"You should. Boys who don't listen to their mamas end up in bad places. You think I ended up in a bad place?"

"No, your place is cool!" Ezra said, jumping into the conversation. Judd nodded in agreement.

"Well, there you go," Finn said, matter-of-factly.

Grant stood up, dusting off his khaki shorts. "Well, should we get home so Ezra can change and we can fill up about a hundred water bottles?"

"Gonna need that many to keep us all hydrated," Olivia said. "I suppose so." She turned to Gracie. "Will we see you again?"

"I'm guessing not. I'll be leaving at about ten tomorrow morning."

"Alright, we'll say our goodbyes now." She stood up, dusting herself off, as Grant had done, then stepped forward to hug Gracie, who stood up to meet her. "It's been so much fun havin' you back, Gracie. It really has. We're gonna miss you."

"Not as much as I'm going to miss you," Gracie said. "I'll be back soon. And you've got my number now. Call me anytime."

"I will," she said.

Gracie turned to Ezra. "Good luck today, bud."

"Thanks," he said, grinning.

She turned to Judd. "You take care of your mama, okay?"

He laughed, his rosy cheeks even more red from the sun's intensity. "That's Daddy's job."

Gracie bent down to his level. "Sometimes mamas need extra love, though, from their babies."

"I'm no baby!" he said, offended.

"I know it. I just meant sometimes the youngest has just the right kind of hugs." He smiled then, and she whispered. "I was the youngest in my family, too."

"Yeah? Alright, I'll take care of Mama."

Olivia smiled behind him, and Grant ruffled his hair. "C'mon you. Let's go," Grant said. They said their goodbyes to Finn, then started to walk away, the boys turned back a gazillion times, waving at them until they disappeared into the parking garage.

"Well, that was fun," Gracie said, sitting back down.

"It was."

"If you say like old times, I might slap you."

"I wasn't going to say that." He sat down beside her, taking a sip from his water bottle. The market had cleared out a bit, but it was still bustling beside them, and Gracie watched people walk by, disappearing into the small tents, and then re-emerging into the sunlight. "So, you're leaving tomorrow?"

"Yeah."

"That was fast."

"I was here a while, Finn. I got a few people to cover my shifts, but they need me back at the hospital."

"I suppose they do."

"You're coming back next month?"

"I think so. For Cayla's birthday."

"It's quite a drive."

She nodded. "I've got to make an effort, you know? I've missed so much. Cayla's so old. I mean, she's not old. She's still a little girl, but if I start missing out on things now, she'll know. She didn't before, but now she will. I can, I don't know, try to redeem myself for not being there. I *want* to be there, ya know? I don't want her to doubt that I love her."

"That's great," he said. He was looking at the grass, not meeting her eyes. She wondered what was going through his head.

"You're far away," she said.

He looked up. "I was just thinking."

"About?"

"Well, us. Could we make it work? Long distance? I mean, I could come up there every other month. You could come down here the others. It could work, couldn't it?"

"You want to date me?" she asked, somewhat flabbergasted.

"Isn't that obvious?"

"You barely know me."

His face grew serious. "That isn't true."

She folded her arms in front of her, studying him. "You're serious?"

"Of course I am."

She sighed. "Finn, I..." What could she say? No, that wasn't the right question. What *should* she say? "I need to be honest with you. You've wanted to know things. Things I've been too afraid to tell you. I haven't been ready to do it. I don't want to do it—tell you, I mean." She paused, closing her eyes. Each time, she'd come close to telling him, she resigned herself to the fact that there was still more time. Now, her time was up. This was it. She had to do it now. "I don't want you to hate me."

"Gracie, I think you think whatever you say is going to be a deal-breaker for me. I'm telling you, nothing you could say is going to change how I feel. How I've always felt." He smiled, averting his eyes. "As stalker-ish as that may sound."

She wanted to smile, too. She would have if she didn't know what she had to say. He'd just told her what she'd always wanted to hear. Instead, her eyes filled up with tears. She looked away, trying her best to keep them from sliding down her cheeks.

"Gracie?"

"You're sweet for saying that."

"Well, I mean it." He sounded upset. "Don't you believe it?"

She looked at him, meeting his eyes, feeling torn. She started to turn away, but he lunged forward, his hands on her face, not letting her look away. "I love you."

She didn't have time to respond before he was kissing her. She felt herself melt into him, and even though she knew she should, she couldn't pull away. When they finally parted, both breathless and dazed, she felt like crying.

"Finn, I was pregnant," she blurted out.

He blinked, taken aback by the words. "When?"

"When I left." She waited for his reply, but he just stared at her. She hung her head, not able to continue looking at him. "We had a daughter, Rosie. She was stillborn." Her tears started to fall, one after the other, in a continuous waterfall. She wiped them away, but they kept coming, sticking to her face instantly because of the extreme heat. When she finally looked up, he wasn't looking at her, but gazing out at the people around them, distracted. Finally, he turned back to her.

"You never told me?" he asked, his voice quieter than Gracie had anticipated.

"I couldn't. Not after what you'd said. I thought you'd think we were ruining your plans. Your life."

"We? You mean you and—" he paused, then looked up at her. "Rosie?"

Gracie froze. She couldn't move. The look on Finn's face was exactly what she'd pictured. Hate. No, revulsion. Or complete abhorrence.

"I was scared. I knew how you felt about getting out of Glenwood."

His face moved in close to hers. She couldn't look away, even though she wanted to. "So, you decided to run away? With my child, no less?" His child. Why did it sound so strange to hear him say it? Rosie was his, too. And he wanted her. He was claiming her. Her heart was pounding, and the nearby smells from the market were now making her feel queasy.

"I was young. Stupid. I didn't want you to hate me like...like..."

"Like what, Gracie? Like what?" His voice was louder, but soft enough not to create a scene.

"Like Daddy hated Mama. For trapping him that way."

Finn shook his head in disgust. "Your dad loved Hannah."

"But not me. He wanted Hannah. He didn't want me. Said Mama tricked him into having me." She hung her head, ashamed.

She felt Finn's eyes on her. The seconds felt like hours as she waited for him to speak. "Everyone has to grow up, Gracie. Get over their shitty childhoods. You could've come back any time, and you didn't."

"I'm here now," she said, moving her hand to place it over his. When he felt it there, he pulled his back, recoiling into himself.

"It all makes sense now. All this time I thought there couldn't be *anything* that bad. *That* awful for you to cut off contact with everyone."

"It was wrong of me," she whispered.

"That's for damn sure." His tone was biting, and each word cut at Gracie like a shard of glass.

"I'm so sorry," she said. She wanted to hug him, comfort him, but his body was turned away and then he stood, looking down at her with that same look of disdain.

"I was a father," he said, his voice sounding far off.

Gracie stood, wiping away more tears. She moved her hands towards her locket, ready to open it, and show him his daughter, but he moved, so fast she didn't have time to react, and grabbed her arms. "This is unforgivable, Gracie." He let go of her just as quickly, turning away and rubbing a hand through his hair once more.

"Finn, I..."

"You knew it was, didn't you?" He spat out, facing her once more. "It's why you waited 'til now to tell me."

She closed her eyes, silently crying for Finn, for Rosie, for the family they'd never be. "I'm so sorry."

"I never want to see you again."

Gracie didn't see him leave. She slumped down against the tree, hiding her face in her hands, trying to stop the shaking, her entire body trembling. An old woman stopped, concerned, and asked if she was alright. She nodded, not looking up, and the woman moved on. Gracie knew she should leave. Why had she told him in such a public place? Why had she told him at all?

When she finally calmed herself enough to walk to her car, the sun was high in the sky. Her eyes were so matted with tears that it hurt to look up so she made her way back, looking at the ground, squinting.

She'd finally been honest—completely honest—and now her heart was breaking all over again.

"Finn, if you're in there, I want you to know that I know what I did was horrible." She paused, breathing in deeply, listening for any sound beyond the door. "I thought about you—and Rosie—every day. Before she was born I almost came back. I should have come back. And after—," she stopped again, remembering the depth of sadness that had swallowed her up until she finally went back to school and immersed herself in classes. "Finn, I'm sorry. I'm so very sorry." She stood, waiting for a response, but there was none. "Goodbye Finn," she whispered.

Walking away this time was almost harder than the last time. Last time she still had Rosie. This time she had no one.

Gracie walked down the stairs and made her way back out into the sunlight. She took her sunglasses out of her purse and put them on, looking both ways for any traffic before scurrying across the street. She was about to climb into her car when she spotted a familiar figure coming down the sidewalk.

"I thought you might be here," Nick said as he approached her.

"You're always following me," Gracie said, almost comforted by the thought. "Of course I'm here. I had to try one last time."

"Didn't go well?"

"He wasn't there. Or didn't answer. One of the two."

Nick looked at her, as if contemplating this. Around them the streets were fairly busy. People walked by, to work meetings or just to take a break from their desks on this beautiful day. Gracie looked up towards Finn's windows, searching for any sign of him, but saw no movement behind the curtains. "Well, listen, I've got something to mull over with you."

"I'm all ears."

"In two weeks I've got some days to take off. I want to come visit you."

A smile spread across Gracie's face and her eyes lit up like fireworks. "Really?"

"Really."

No one had ever been to visit Gracie. Not that they wouldn't have, but this was something. A few days ago, she didn't even know she had a brother, and now he was offering to drive half a day—or night, if he drove the way Gracie did—just to see her. It felt wonderful, and she felt undeserving.

"You really want to do that?" she asked.

"Of course I do." He smiled, too, nudging her shoulder. "I've been waiting for the day to meet my kid sis. Now that I have—well, I guess I kind of like her."

"You have two kid sisters, you know. And the other one lives much closer."

"I know. And I need to tell her the truth about who I am."

"You do."

"The thing is, Gracie, I've spent time with her family and your mom. I know Hannah. I want to know you, too."

Even though it was just a statement, a fact of his life, it felt very much like a compliment, too. "Nick Tooley, you are more than welcome to come visit me if you want to make the drive."

He moved forward, wrapping his arms around her. "I'll be there. I'll give you a call in a few days when I know my schedule for sure.

"That sounds perfect." She squeezed her arms tightly around him, and she felt, for the first time since they'd met, an undeniable protectiveness radiating from him. It must be how all little sisters felt in the presence of their older brother. All Gracie knew was that it felt right.

"So, you need me to go up and kick some sense into the guy?" he asked, gesturing towards Finn's building.

"No need for that. I think I've kicked him where it hurts quite enough."

They were both quiet for a minute, and then Nick spoke again. "You've got to forgive yourself, too."

"Does that really matter if he doesn't forgive me?"

Nick leaned back, resting his shoulders on the top of Gracie's car. "You know it does."

Gracie leaned back next to him, crossing her arms in front of her. "You're always giving me advice. You only just met me. I'm beginning to wonder if you do this with everyone you know."

He laughed, crossing his arms, too. "I suppose I do. I'm a cop. Heck, it's what I do every day."

"Trying to keep people out of trouble, huh?"

"Something like that."

"I thought I had, you know," she said, dropping her arms to her sides. "Forgiven myself."

"It's a hard thing to do."

"It is, Nick. Damn hard. But you know what? You're right. I need to do it. I've told the truth the best that I can. I've been honest with everyone here. If things are over after all that, then there's nothing else I can do."

"That's right."

She looked up at him. Their eyes met and he took her hand in his. "And I've got you," she said.

"You do," he agreed. "And you've got Hannah."

"That's right."

"What more could you want?" he asked, a lopsided grin on his face.

Her heart knew the answer, but now her head told her it might finally be time to move on and to let go of Finn Miller.

◗ 15.

FINN WAS IN THE KITCHEN WHEN HE HEARD THE KNOCK ON the door. His heart raced in his chest, and he didn't move toward it right away. He knew before he even heard her voice that it was Gracie.

Slowly, he walked over to it, glancing out of the peephole.

It was strange, finally knowing the whole truth. He'd been waiting for it for ten years, and in all that time, considering all the scenarios, he'd never anticipated the truth.

"Finn?" Gracie said through the door.

He reached out, his hand grazing the wood. He leaned into it, not making a sound.

How had it come to this? How could so much of him want to fling open the door and take her in his arms while the other part wanted to lash out, hurt her the way she'd just hurt him.

"Finn, if you're in there, I want you to know that I know what I did was horrible."

He looked out the peephole again. She had rested her head below it and was leaning on the door so he almost couldn't see her at all. He pushed himself off the door, backing away, looking at it, unsure of what to do.

"I thought about you—and Rosie—every day. Before she was born I almost came back. I should have come back. And after—," She'd stopped talking. He kept his body still, waiting. "Finn, I'm sorry. I'm so very sorry."

When he looked down, his hands were trembling. How could she have such an effect on him? It infuriated him. He'd tried to move on so many times. He'd dated, had more than a few relationships that could have—should have—progressed into something more. He'd tried to forget her. Or had he? He sang about her every time he picked up his guitar. He remembered her all the time. And a few days ago, when he saw her in that hotel lobby, he'd known that he'd never gotten over her completely.

As kids, he and Gracie had learned to walk, run in tandem. They'd hit, kicked, yelled at each other every day then hugged, kissed, run through the yard chasing each other in fits of laughter. It was like they were siblings, but even as a kid, Finn had never felt related to Gracie Brannen. As they grew older, her rough and tumble ways drew him to her more. While all the other girls seemed more interested in hair and makeup, Gracie wanted to lose herself fishing by the pond. She'd never quite fit in, and that's what Finn had liked about her. By the time they were teenagers, Finn had accepted his feelings for her as more than just friends. When other guys started taking notice, it bothered him. Gracie'd had no idea, thinking they all had eyes for Hannah.

He remembered how it had started, the two of them not so young anymore, admitting their feelings for each other. They'd been swimming with a group of kids from school. It was late in the summer, and they'd been in the pond all day, soaking up the sun and enjoying the feeling of the cool water between their toes. Tired and out of breath, Gracie emerged from the water, falling to the ground, breathing hard, looking up at the sky. Finn had sat down beside her to catch his breath and they silently watched the others laughing from the water.

"You want to go out with me some time, Gracie?" he asked. He'd wanted to ask for weeks.

"Go out where?" she said, closing her eyes.

"Like on a date," he mumbled.

"Huh?" Wide-eyed she'd sat up and pushed his shoulder, knocking his arm back. "We can't date. What if we break up?"

"Why would we break up?" It was an innocent question on Finn's part. He'd had no experience with dating, though he'd noticed pretty girls here and there. But he'd only ever been interested in Gracie, and the thought of her starting to date someone else, as kids were prone to do at their age, told him he couldn't put off asking her any longer.

She shrugged. "Everybody breaks up. We're awful young, Finn. What if you met somebody else?"

"Like who?"

"I don't know. Somebody."

He didn't think there was anybody else to meet who would get his heart racing like just seeing Gracie Brannen smile did.

"How would you even drive us? You don't turn 16 for another few months."

"We don't have to drive somewhere for a date."

"Isn't that the point of a date?" she asked.

"Nah, it's to get to know someone."

"We already know each other, Finn."

"Alright, well it's to get to know them in a different way, see if there's a spark, ya know?"

She'd been quiet for a moment, and to his surprise she'd turned quite serious.

"You don't know I already love you?" she had asked, turning her face away. He'd never seen her so willingly vulnerable, opening herself up like that. It made her even more beautiful to him.

He smiled. "I guess I do now."

She'd looked at him, finally, searching his eyes for something. "Just don't hurt me, Finn."

He hadn't responded, just pulled her face to his and kissed her there. It had only taken a few seconds for the rest of the group to begin whooping and hollering around them, and Gracie had pulled away, blushing.

"Was that your first kiss?" Grant yelled, slapping the water with his hands.

"Aw, shut up, Grant," Finn yelled back, but there was a big smile on his face.

"Well, it's about time, you two." Olivia added, before diving back in.

"Don't stop on account of us," a boy named Devon said. A few of the other girls they were with whispered to each other.

Finn had looked over at Gracie, but she was no longer embarrassed. In fact, she looked damn proud to have kissed him.

They'd been inseparable after that, even more so than before. They spent hours talking about their future together, what they wanted from life. And then, bam, he woke up one morning, went to her house and Hannah, her eyes red from crying, had told him she was gone.

Now, he knew why.

He walked back to the kitchen, pouring himself a shot of whiskey. Finn liked the taste of it, always had, and drank it down quickly, the warm liquid running down his throat. He poured himself another, then sat down at the table.

For the past decade all he'd thought about was why. Why had Gracie Brannen left him? After everything, why had she been so cruel? He'd wanted to give her everything, everything he knew she thought she didn't deserve. Instead, he'd worked himself to the bone through the years, trying to forget her. Trying not to think about the family she could be creating with someone else while he himself had none, unable to move on without any answers from the one girl he'd always loved.

Tilting his head back, he drank down the second shot in one big gulp.

As it turned out, he *had* had a family.

16.

CAYLA PLACED ONE OF HER DOLLS ON THE TOP OF HER suitcase before she zipped it up. "Take it with you," she said. "And bring it back every time you come back so we can have a visit, Dolly and I."

Gracie's heart dropped. "I'll be back so much, you won't even have time to miss me," she said. Then, Cayla ran from the room, tears in her eyes, to Dave, waiting to take her to her last day of camp.

The night before she'd slept fitfully, her mind unable to shut down and rest. She'd known all along that she had to be honest with Finn before returning to Pomroy. It had left her mind racing, her heart pounding in her ears, and as she lay counting backwards, counting sheep, staring at the ceiling even, she went back, over and over, to Finn's face.

Now the deed was done, and she wanted to curl up in her older sister's arms and sleep for days, but she had a long drive ahead of her and much to think about.

"Gracie," Hannah said after Cayla and Dave had gone. "All set?"

"Yep." Gracie took a deep breath and let out a sigh.

"And you saw Finn?"

"Mm-hmm."

"And?"

"It's over. Maybe it's always been over."

"You told him?"

Gracie nodded. "He never wants to see me again."

"Surely he was just angry."

"Angry? He was furious. I've never seen him like that. He's never looked at me that way before. With such disgust."

Hannah's fingers stroked Gracie's hair. "Now, now. It was a shock is all. You'll see."

"No, H. This is it. He's got his reason to let me go now. I suppose it's partly why I never came back to tell him."

"And hiding away didn't bring you peace, did it? Trust me, you will feel that now that you've let go of this secret. You loved Finn enough to tell him the truth."

"How do you know, H? Because, to be perfectly honest with you, all I feel is despair and hopelessness."

Hannah turned to face her on the couch. She took Gracie's hand and cupped it in hers. "I know because love is everything. If we didn't have it, then what are we doing here? What would be the point of all of this?"

"He might never get past it. How does that make it better? I could have kept this to myself and had a life with him. You know that, right? He wanted us to be together."

"And it never would have lasted. You knew that. You can't begin a relationship with secrets and lies hanging between you."

"I never lied," Gracie said.

"No, you never lied." Hannah agreed. "You just ran."

"Am I doing it again?"

"I'm hopeful that you're not. I want to see you again. I'd like us to be close. I miss you when you're not here."

Gracie pulled her sister to her, burying her head into her shoulder. She didn't want to let go. "I love you, Hannah."

"You never call me that."

"Maybe I want to make sure you know it's true."

It seemed sometimes that words were insufficient. Why were goodbyes so hard? It had to be, in part, because there was no way to say everything you wanted to say.

Everything you needed to say. And what if there wasn't another chance?

"You'll be back in a few weeks, right?"

Gracie nodded.

"See how things go once you get back. Maybe Finn will reach out. He may just need some time."

"I know. What you're saying makes sense, but my heart feels like it's the end."

"It could be, I suppose." Hannah hadn't said it to be mean, but her honesty was distressing. "Listen, even if this is it for you and Finn, that doesn't mean that you won't find happiness."

"I can't picture a future without him in it."

Hannah was quiet a moment. She got up, went to the kitchen and came back holding a photo. It had wrinkled and faded with time, but as she handed it to Gracie, the faces were clear as day. Four friends leaning against Mama's old house—Olivia's arm was flung around Gracie, who was pushing away Finn's face with her hand. Grant had hold of one of Finn's legs, his mouth wide open like he'd been laughing. They must have been around nine or so in the photo. "What's this?"

"Something Mama had. She said she looked at it whenever she missed you. Said it made her happy to remember you that way."

Staring at the photo, Gracie could see why. She could feel the joy of that day.

Hannah crossed her arms in front of her. "I don't think Finn's ever thought of a life without you in it, either. Don't give up just yet."

"Can I take this?" she asked, looking up at Hannah.

"Of course."

She tucked the photo into her purse, then stood.

"Call me when you get back?"

"I will," she said. "What about you? Will you be alright?"

"I always am." Hannah mustered up a smile.

"I'm serious, H." She knew Hannah liked to put on a brave face.

"Dave never should have told you about Dr. Taft," she said, rolling her eyes.

"I'm glad he did."

"Well, don't you worry about me. As long as we get to see you every once in a while and hear from you, we'll be okay. Just don't go disappearing on us again, you hear?"

"I won't." She picked up her bag and moved for the door. "Bye, H."

It was late when Gracie walked through the door to her apartment, or early depending on how you looked at it. She dropped her bags on the floor upon entering and flipped on a light. The place was just as she left it, but it felt different somehow—quieter.

Rubbing her eyes, she made her way to the bathroom. Her eyes heavy, she took out her contacts and slipped on her glasses before walking to the bedroom. She pulled back the covers and climbed into bed. While she was excited to get back to work in the morning, she was exhausted. Her body had been through the ringer today, both physically and emotionally, and she was drained.

A faint glow came from the living room, and she remembered setting her phone on the counter. It would need to be charged overnight, and she needed to let Hannah know she'd gotten home safe. Reluctantly, she forced herself out of bed to retrieve it.

Once it was plugged in, she sent Hannah a text. *Made it home. Long drive. I'll call you after work tomorrow.*

Olivia had sent her an email, so she clicked it open, finding several photos from the barbecue on the farm. One of her and Judd eating her apple pie. A few Grant must have taken of her and Olivia as they sat talking on the deck. And the last one was her and Finn, sitting next to the fire.

She realized, after looking through the photos, that she missed it, the simplicity of life in Glenwood. She missed the ease of laughing with her old friends and slipping into the friendships that had shaped her. Once upon a time she'd been dead set on leaving it all behind, then she'd felt like she had to. Now, she wasn't sure what she felt.

Olivia's note was short.

> It was great to see you, G. Don't be a stranger. We loved having you back in Glenwood. Print one of these off and stick it to the fridge so you remember to come back and visit!

She'd ended it with a winky face.

Gracie set her phone down and rolled over, tucking her legs up behind her knees. She closed her eyes, willing her mind to shut off. She didn't want to think about anything. Not Finn's face when she told him about Rosie. Not the tears in Cayla's eyes when she left.

She wanted it to all fade away.

Instead, their faces lingered in her mind.

The bed in 341 had been occupied for months, the patient a stout girl who hated the hospital, the staff, and the food, everything about being there. Gracie had been sympathetic, knowing how hard it must have been for the girl to be missing out on her life, stuck in a temporary bed, a temporary room, her life on hold.

So she was surprised when she entered the room to find her patient gone, and a new one in her place.

The young boy looked up at her when she came in, and she quickly grabbed his chart from the end of the bed. It had been a challenge getting back into her groove here at St. Claire's Children's Hospital, her mind constantly thinking of all the people she'd left behind.

"Peter Kinney," she said, looking up over the clipboard.

"That's me," he said without sitting up. In fact, he simply continued to stare out the window.

The boy had been hit by a car as he rode his bike out of his driveway, resulting in a broken arm and a stay in the hospital so they could administer a CT scan and monitor him for a bleed.

"I'm Gracie," she said, watching him. How are you feeling this morning?" she asked.

He shrugged.

"Not too happy about being here?"

"I don't care about being here," he pointed to his arm with his good hand. "Can't play the rest of the summer."

"Baseball?" she asked.

He nodded. "Second base."

"Bet you're a pretty good batter, too."

"Three homeruns this season already."

"Wow," Gracie said, impressed. "Well, you'll be back out there in no time."

"It'll be weeks won't it?"

She looked down at his chart. "You fractured it at the growth plate. It'll require some long-term care to ensure the joint surface and the plate align correctly."

He looked at her as if she was speaking another language.

"You'll want to listen to..." She looked back down at his chart. "Dr. Norman's advice. Don't go thinking you're Superman."

He laughed at that. "Obviously I'm not."

She smirked, raising an eyebrow at him. "Three homeruns this season, you said? I'd say that takes some sort of superpower."

"Yeah, I guess so."

"How old are you, Peter?"

"Thirteen."

"Well, you've got plenty of summers left for baseball."

He looked out the window. She wondered if he was thinking of all the games he would be missing out on.

"Parents here?" she asked, changing the subject.

"They had to get back to work. They're stopping by later with my little brother." He looked at Gracie. "*He* gets to play baseball the rest of the summer, and I'll be stuck in the stands watching him."

She felt bad for the kid. She remembered being that young, the future too far off to think about in any tangible way. He didn't care that he'd be able to play next summer. Next summer might as well be ten years from now. Or forty. All he could think about was right now. And right now, she suspected, looked pretty damn miserable.

Still...she bent down so she was leaning on the bed, more on his level. "Support your brother," she said. She waited for him to meet her eyes. "How else will he learn to support you?"

He didn't respond, but he didn't need to. She knew he understood. Turning on her heel, she quickly jotted down the time on his chart. "Just press that button if you need anything, Peter."

"Thanks," he mumbled.

Gracie stared out the window, watching the commotion of the city on the ground below. Cars sped off to their next appointments. People jaywalked hurriedly through traffic. She gathered up her things before making her way down to Peter's room, thinking of the way he'd stared out the window, sad and confused by the accident that had changed all his summer plans.

She knew how Peter felt. He would be missing out on his life. On moments he could never get back. The same way she had missed out on a million different moments over the course of the last ten years.

She stepped into the room.

"Peter?" she asked, tentatively.

He looked up as she approached. A man and a woman stood beside the bed, and a younger boy was playing by the window, flying a toy airplane into it and letting it crash onto the windowsill.

"You feeling any better?"

He nodded. "These are my parents," he said. The woman stepped forward to shake her hand. "And that's my little brother, George."

"Hello, George."

"Mom, Dad, this is my nurse, Gracie."

"It's nice to meet you," Peter's dad said before walking over to the lone armchair in the room and sitting down.

"Peter, I'm going to run down to that little shop and get some coffee. Can I get you anything?"

"No, I'm fine. Thanks, Mom."

She walked around Gracie quickly and exited the room.

"The woman needs her coffee," Mr. Kinney chuckled. He'd taken out his phone and was punching something into it.

"My mom drinks like ten cups a day," Peter said, rolling his eyes.

George Kinney came bounding over from the window. He looked up at Gracie with wide eyes, then pointed over Gracie's shoulder. "What's that do?"

"That's a patient monitor. It gives us an idea of how the patient is doing."

"Can't you just look at 'em and see?"

Gracie smiled. "Sometimes. But you can't see what's going on inside the body, so those machines can help alert us to those things."

He nodded, trying to understand.

"So, you're Peter's little brother? Peter told me all about you and how excited he is to watch you play baseball this summer."

George looked surprised, and Mr. Kinney looked up from his phone. "He did?" George asked.

"He did." Gracie looked over at Peter who offered a faint smile. "Since he won't be able to hit any more homeruns this summer, he's hoping you can hit some. You know, to keep the Kinney family records coming."

George blushed and looked at the floor before stealing a glance at Peter.

"Yeah, George," Peter said. "I can give you some pointers if you want."

"Really?" Gracie turned, hearing Mr. Kinney's voice. "Yesterday you didn't even want to go to George's games."

George's eyes moved from his older brother to his dad, and back again, waiting patiently to see where the conversation would go.

"Yeah, but Dad, if I don't support George, he won't learn how to support anyone else." He looked at Gracie out of the corner of his eyes, then turned his attention back to his dad. "He's really going to count on me this summer."

Mr. Kinney smiled. "I'm really glad to hear that, Peter."

"Me too," George said, crawling up on his big brother's bed. The two boys snuggled up together and George cupped his hands around his mouth and said, louder than he intended, "This is gonna be a great summer, Peter."

Peter nodded. "Yes, George. Yes, it is."

Before Gracie turned to walk out, she saw Mr. Kinney put down his phone. By the time she opened the door, he was sitting on Peter's bed, the three of them going over George's end-of-summer baseball game plan.

17.

"I THOUGHT YOU'D SAID YOU'D LIVED HERE A LONG TIME."

Gracie looked up from the stack of mail she was carrying. "I have."

Nick glanced around at the blank white walls, the sparse furniture and the few boxes in the corner of the apartment. "How long?"

"Two years."

"You've lived here two years and you've never hung anything up? What are those boxes over there?" He asked, pointing to the disheveled corner. The boxes were partially open as if someone had opened them, looking for something, but hadn't wanted to break the seal completely.

"Oh, those? They're just some books. I think my alarm clock is in one of them. Some picture frames. You know. Just stuff."

"Why didn't you put the frames out?"

Gracie shrugged. "I don't know."

"Well, I can see why you don't like being here much. It's not homey at all."

"Eh, it's just a place to sleep."

As Gracie walked into the kitchen, she set the mail down on the counter. Opening a cupboard she took out some corn flakes and poured herself a bowl. "Want some?"

"Nah. Not much for cereal."

She raised an eyebrow at that, but continued fixing her bowl. "Anyway, what's your place like?"

"Back in Ashland?" He sat down on the couch, leaning back and putting his hands behind his head. "It's an old house I rent with a buddy.

"Yeah? And it's homey?" She joined him in the living room, taking a bite of her cereal.

"It's got some great wall colors." Nick put his hands down and began waving them around as he spoke. He was a very animated guy, which was strange to see. Once she'd figured out that he was her brother, her father's son, she'd started noticing the resemblance more. His personality, which was very open and accepting, crashed right into whatever looks and expressions he shared with her daddy. "Trey, my roommate, he's an aspiring novelist, so we've got piles of books everywhere. And my dog, Batman, lives there, too, so his toys are all over the place."

"Cute name. What kind of dog is he?"

"A boxer."

"Aren't those pretty big?" she asked, wrinkling her nose.

"They are."

"Your place is big enough for him?"

"Uh-huh. That's what I'm saying. It might not be the largest space, but it's got everything I need. It's somewhere I like coming home to. It feels good to walk through the door every night when I get off at the station."

Gracie thought about this. "So you're saying I don't like coming home to this place because I don't have a dog and a few books out?" He had to be joking.

"I'm saying it doesn't look like this is a place you've been living in for long, but you've been here for two years. That just surprised me."

"So I need a roommate? Or someone to help me make messes?"

He laughed. "I guess I'm thinking maybe you never wanted to get comfortable here."

Gracie put her spoon down, clinking it into the bowl and splashing some milk as she set the bowl down on the coffee table. "Did Mama ever tell you about my backpack?"

Nick shook his head.

"I had this old bag, probably used to be Mama or Daddy's at some point, but I'd found it and carried it around with me everywhere. I'd put anything you could think of inside it. Rocks. Books. Clothes. One day—I must've been about four—Mama took it off my back and opened it up. She asked me why I wanted to lug around all this stuff. She said 'stuff' like it was all just a bunch of crap, ya know. And maybe it was."

Nick leaned forward, his elbows resting on his knees. "What did you say?"

"I said I wanted to be ready if we ever had to go. I didn't want it to be a surprise."

"Go where?"

"Away." Gracie closed her eyes, remembering. "I mean, I was four years old. I already knew then that something was wrong with our family." She looked up at Nick.

He licked his lips. "You know, I was always jealous of you. That time I saw you at the fair. You looked so happy. Your dad didn't look that bad from my viewpoint."

"Well, you didn't see him later."

"I know. What I'm trying to say is I always thought you had it so great. Your parents were together. Mine weren't. But the more I get to know you, Gracie, the more I think I was the lucky one."

She thought about this. "Your mom never remarried?"

"There were always guys around. I mean, she was with *him*, so you know she didn't have great taste in men."

"But no one you could look up to?"

"No, I think that's why I was so curious about him."

"How many times did you see him?"

"Only a handful. By the time he saw me at the fair, he'd made it clear that he wanted nothing to do with me." Nick stood up and walked across the room. "Mind if I get a glass of water?"

"Oh no," Gracie said. "Help yourself."

"Do you ever wonder what happened to him?" Nick asked when he'd returned to the sofa.

"Not really."

"No?" Nick asked, surprised.

"No. I probably fucked up everything in my life partially because of him. I mean, everything was my choice. I admit that. But I do blame him for a lot of it."

"Do you really think you fucked up *everything*?"

"Nick, Finn won't answer any of my texts. None of my calls. He told me he wanted to be with me. When I was honest with him, he ran. It doesn't get much clearer than that."

"If he loves you, he'll be back."

"Oh, really? Do you want to know why I left?" She sat forward in her chair. "I was pregnant. Finn and I were going to be parents." She took in his reaction, but he didn't seem as surprised as she expected. She went on. "The night before I left I asked him what he thought of having kids. I didn't tell him I was pregnant then. Just asked, you know, out of curiosity. It was clear that he didn't want them. At least not right away. And I didn't want to end up like Mama, with a husband who resented his family. I couldn't bear it. To live that way after I'd hated Mama for making us do it. And then, I gave birth to Rosie. Perfect Rosie."

"But she never took a breath on her own," Gracie continued. "She was stillborn." Gracie wiped a tear away. "I'd told myself that I'd tell him once she was here, but I don't even know if that was true. I left so my baby wouldn't have to feel what I felt as a child—unwanted. After she was born, I didn't want anyone to know. I didn't want them to taint her. She was all I had been holding onto, and then when I left the hospital without her..." Gracie choked back a sob. "I couldn't tell him then. That he'd been a father, but that now there was no little girl for him to hold."

"I'm sorry, Gracie." He said, at last.

Gracie stood up and walked to the window. Her eyes were shining, and she tenderly touched the necklace hanging around her neck. A few clouds rolled by, covering up the sun and turning the apartment dark around them. She knew Nick was watching her—waiting. She wanted to tell him more about Rosie. How her skin had been almost translucent. Her hair softer than a chenille sweater. Her tiny fingers, unable to grasp at Gracie, but beautiful just the same. And how her lips, which should have been a soft pink, were instead purple. But she couldn't speak. She turned back to face him. "I've had a lot of time to come to terms with it. Finn hasn't. But if someone told you what I told Finn, would you forgive them?"

He didn't say anything, and Gracie knew what he was thinking.

"You have to remember," he said, finally. "We share the same father. I've got a stubborn streak a hundred years strong—same as you. From what you've told me about Finn, he's pretty fond of you. If that's really the case, I wouldn't count him out."

Gracie relaxed, filled with a renewed sense of hope by his words. The afternoon had been pleasant. She found she really enjoyed Nick's company, and they did have a lot in common. She walked back and sat beside him, taking hold of his hand, clasping hers around it. "Thank you, Nick. I don't know if you're right. I may never see him again. He has every right to shut me out." It was true. She agreed with Finn's actions. Hell, if it had been her, she'd have put as much distance between them as possible and gone at least another ten years without seeing him or uttering his name.

"We all make mistakes," he said.

She nodded. "I know it's true, but it feels like I'm the one with all the atoning to do."

Nick put his other hand behind her head, bringing it down and kissing the top of it softly. "It might feel like that now. Listen, you've taken a big step. You've told the truth. You went back to Glenwood. You faced everything you were afraid of and came out of it in one piece. He smiled, and, through her tears, Gracie couldn't help but smile back.

"I like having you here," she said.

"Of course you do. No one likes to be alone all the time."

When Finn had left her at the market, she'd felt what she had when she'd had to say goodbye to Rosie. At some point, years later, she had started to come out of her self-made cocoon, slowly immersing herself back into the world. She'd quit her waitressing job, stopped drinking away her sadness at whatever bar her co-workers trounced off to after closing each night, and began to think seriously about what she was going to do with the rest of her life. She'd let herself finally feel hopeful, the same as she felt now, sitting here with Nick.

"I've made so many mistakes," she said, breathing in and sighing deeply.

Nick was still holding her hand when he looked into her eyes and said, "Just let them go. You can hate yourself or love yourself, but if you want this brother, right here, to stick around, you're going to start loving yourself and accepting the choices you made, even though you might not agree with them now. You feel guilty because you're a different person now than you were then. And that's a good thing. You've grown. Gracie, you should remember your daughter in a good light, not in this guilt-ridden way that you remember her now."

"Nick Tooley," she said, charmed by his words.

"Yes?"

"Promise you'll always be my brother."

"I always have been, haven't I?"

"But I didn't know it then."

He smiled. "I promise."

She took a deep breath and hugged him, taking care not to notice how similar his embrace felt to her daddy's. They had the same body type, but Gracie could attest to the fact that the similarities ended there. His build was the only thing he shared with his biological father. Nick Tooley was nothing, if not honorable.

"She's beautiful." The nurse leaned over, peering at the bundle in Gracie's arms. Gracie looked up, caught off guard by the comment. "I'm Stella," she said. "I helped deliver her."

Gracie didn't know what to say. She looked up briefly then whispered, "Thank you."

"Did you name her?" Nurse Stella asked, laying a hand on Gracie's shoulder.

Gracie nodded. "Rosie."

The nurse smiled, and even though talking with this woman was the last thing she wanted to do right now, in the absence of her family, it felt nice to have someone ask about her baby. She'd given birth more than three hours ago after a long, arduous labor. She remembered seeing Stella's face as she pushed, bent down close near the doctor as Rosie was born. Surely, her shift had ended, but here she stood, a comfort to Gracie now. She looked up from Rosie into Stella's brown eyes. Her hair was in a messy bun, and she looked as if she could have been the same age as Mama. She wasn't sure what compelled her to say her next words, but it could have been that close resemblance. "Would you sit with us for a minute?"

Stella immediately took a seat on the bed, facing Gracie. "I'll stay as long as you need me to."

Gracie turned back to Rosie, stroking her cheek and feeling the baby soft skin of her daughter's cheek. She hadn't stopped crying since they put Rosie in her arms. Even now, when she thought she must have cried all the tears she had, they fell from her eyes like droplets from a leaky faucet. When she looked back up, she saw Stella was also crying. The two women, virtual strangers, sat together for another hour, saying nothing, each of them mourning the loss of the little girl in Gracie's arms.

"She looks like Finn," Gracie said. She didn't care that Stella didn't know who Finn was. "His eyes and mouth."

Stella moved so she could see Rosie's face. "Look at those long fingers. Same as yours."

"A pianist's fingers."

Stella smiled. "Or a surgeon's."

So many hopes and dreams, thought Gracie. Just gone. She could almost see Rosie playing the piano as a young girl if she focused on it enough. She even pictured Finn sitting next to her on the bench, playing his guitar.

"How do I let go of her?" she asked.

A tear rolled down Stella's face. "You don't have to. She is still your daughter, whether she is physically with you or not."

Gracie thought about that. It made her feel stronger to know she didn't have to say goodbye. She couldn't have, anyway, even if she'd tried.

"I've never loved anyone this much," she said, more to Rosie than to Stella, but the nurse nodded.

"The love you feel when you become a mother is unlike anything else."

Gracie's heart plummeted in her chest. "Am I a mother?" She would be leaving the hospital without her child. To everyone out in the world, she wouldn't be a mother.

"Do you love Rosie?" Stella asked, her eyes wide.

"With all my heart."

"Are you proud of her?"

"I am," Gracie said, looking down at Rosie's face. At closed eyes that would never flutter open. At a mouth that would never cry out in hunger or fear, or giggle at her mama's funny faces. The stillness was what Gracie would remember later.

"Then, I think you know that you are a mother."

Gracie nodded.

When she finally said goodbye to Rosie, Stella was there. And when she walked from her hospital room to go home, Stella was there. "Do you have a car here?" she asked. Gracie shook her head. Her roommate, Laura, had dropped her off on her way to work. "Let me drive you," she said, holding out her hand.

Gracie took it, letting Stella lead her out of the maternity ward, down the elevator and out of the building to her car. Gracie gave her the directions as she stared out the window. They pulled up to the apartment building where Gracie was subleasing a room. The apartment belonged to two other girls, and she'd just planned to stay a few months until she could afford her own one-bedroom for her and Rosie. Now, it looked like that wasn't happening.

"Do you have roommates?" Stella asked before they got out of the car.

Gracie nodded, hoping they weren't home. She couldn't bear the thought of telling them she'd gone into labor early and that Rosie hadn't made it.

"How about if I go up, pack up a few things for you, and you can stay with me for a while?"

"What?"

"It's no problem." Stella said, waiting for her answer.

Gracie fished her keys out of her pocket, handing them over to Stella. "It's this one," she said, pointing out the correct key. "My room is the closest to the front door. There's a bag on the floor of the closet."

"I'll be back in a jiffy." Stella said, taking the keys and climbing out of the car. Gracie watched as she made her way into the building. The weather had started growing colder in recent weeks. In a few days, it would be Thanksgiving. She'd thought maybe she'd return home with Rosie. Hannah had been emailing more than usual since she'd left, asking if she'd be coming back for the holiday.

"It'd make Mama really happy if you did," Hannah had emailed her. "We'll make a turkey and everything. Not watch football. Decorate the Christmas tree. It'll be perfect. Think about it, Gracie. You know, Finn came around asking about you. He wants to know where you are—to make sure you're alright. We all miss you. Come home, Gracie. Please, come home."

She should go home. She barely had enough money to live off of. She had no one here. Her roommates were just that, not interested in her life story, and she supposed she wasn't too interested in theirs either. It had been an arrangement of convenience and that was all. If she went home, Mama would hold her, comfort her. Hannah would lead her in the right direction to get on with her life. But, would it be her life? She'd never wanted to stay in Glenwood.

Stella returned, breaking her from her thoughts. She opened the door and handed a bag to Gracie. "One of your roommates was there. I just said I was a friend, getting some things for you and that you'd be staying with me for a few days. I gave her my number in case she needs to get a hold of you, but she didn't seem too concerned about it. Are you guys close?"

"No, we just live together."

"I thought so." Stella said, adjusting herself as she sat back down in the driver's seat. "I grabbed what I thought you might need. Honestly, I'm guessing you'll just want to sleep the next few days."

Gracie didn't ask, but she wondered how Stella knew what she would want. She didn't even know for sure herself.

Later that night, Gracie slipped on her pajamas and walked out to the living room of Stella's small bungalow. It was quite old, with a separate dining and living room. Stella joined her a few minutes later, handing her a hand-knit quilt. "Here, wrap yourself up in this," she said. "I suppose fall is on its way out, and winter is gearing up. These low ceilings help trap the heat. This place stays pretty warm, but you might like having this, too."

Grateful, Gracie took the quilt, wrapping it around her shoulders. "Did you make this?" she asked as Stella took a seat on the sofa. Gracie pulled the blanket tight around her and sat beside her.

"Oh heavens no. I don't know how to knit." Stella reached over and felt the corner of the blanket. Her eyelids were heavy and her face was serious. "A volunteer group delivered these to the hospital when my A.J. was born."

"A.J.? You have a son?" Stella hadn't mentioned it at all today. Gracie tried to remember if she had said anything about him at the hospital, but she couldn't recall hearing his name.

"Had. I had a son. He passed away."

"I'm so sorry," Gracie said, everything becoming clearer. Stella had offered her a hand because she'd been in Gracie's shoes. Of course she had. When Stella had sat by her side, not saying a word, she'd felt so grateful. Stella had known in that moment she'd needed someone with her. Someone else to acknowledge the tragedy she'd endured, but to also know that she couldn't speak, couldn't move.

"It happened over twenty years ago," she said as she flipped on the TV. The volume was down and she left it that way. A habit for someone needing company that Gracie was familiar with as well, the voices in the tube providing background noise, making it feel less lonely. "My husband and I lost him to SIDS. He was eight months old." She breathed out deeply. "William—my husband—fell apart. After a while, we were strangers to each other. I had to leave so I wouldn't be swallowed up, too. William went to a dark place in the days after A.J. passed. I tried to bring him back, but..." Her voice trailed off.

Gracie sucked in her breath, thinking of Finn. What would have happened if they had lost their child together? If he knew? Would it have torn them apart anyway? She couldn't picture Finn a stranger. Thinking of him that way was painful, but wasn't that what he was now? "Is that why you're helping me?" Gracie asked after a while.

"I don't know, actually," Stella said. "My shift had ended before Rosie even came, giving me three whole days off, but when we realized there was no heartbeat, and you had no one with you..." Stella met her eyes. "I just had to stay."

And now, here she was, spending her vacation days taking in a stranger who'd just lost a child.

"Thank you." Gracie met her eyes.

She smiled. "You said that already."

"I just want to make sure you know how grateful I am."

Stella shifted on the couch, "Ah, honey, you don't even need to think twice about it."

Gracie smiled politely.

Her eyelids grew heavier with each passing moment. She wanted to close them, but she was afraid. What if she woke up and forgot Rosie's face? What if her only memory of her daughter vanished into her dream world? Before she knew it, tears had pooled in the corners of her eyes and she couldn't help the uncontrollable sobbing that came next. Stella sat up, putting an arm on her back, slowly rubbing it in a circular motion. "There, there," she murmured, her voice low and deep.

By the time Gracie had stopped crying, Stella had moved to the kitchen, bringing back hot tea and setting it down on the coffee table in front of her.

"Will it always feel like this?" she asked, before moving her hands out of the blanket and picking up the warm cup.

"Feel like what, honey?"

"Like I'm getting hit by a truck, over and over. It's like I can't move from its path. I'm scared, and then terrified, and then I'm looking around wondering what the hell happened."

Stella gave her a sympathetic look. Her face was worn, probably from the long shift at the hospital, but Gracie guessed it was also because of her line of work. It had to be exhausting, taking a toll on her body. "You'll probably feel like that for a long, long time."

"Will I forget her?" Gracie asked, holding back another sob. "I can't forget her."

"You won't." Stella said. "Did they give you a picture of her?"

Gracie nodded. "They did."

Stella stood up and disappeared down the hallway. When she returned she was holding a gold locket. "Here," she said, holding it out to Gracie. "I wore this for years, so I could keep A.J. close to my heart. Whenever I felt my memories were slipping, I just opened it up. Just seeing his face brought a smile to mine, and I'd start remembering things about him."

"But, I can't take this," Gracie said, pushing the locket back toward Stella.

"It's alright. I don't need it anymore. I haven't worn it in years. I've looked at it so much that photo is implanted in my memory."

Gracie conceded, taking the locket into her hands. She got up, moving to pick up her purse, which she'd dropped at the door when they came in. She felt around for the photo, pulling it out and smiling at the sight of it. Rosie. Her Rosie. How silly it was to think she could ever forget. Stella was behind her, holding out a pair of scissors. Gracie took them and cut the image down before placing it in the small locket. While not quite a perfect fit, it did the job, and, more than anything, it soothed Gracie, knowing she could look down, open the locket and see Rosie's face.

After Stella had gone to bed and Gracie lay, holding tight to the locket while tears trickled down her face, her mind wandered as she drifted off to sleep. She saw a young girl, her eyes wide, and her hair bouncing along behind her as she skipped around Gracie. Come with me, the girl said, laughing. It was Rosie. It had to be. I want to, baby. I want to so bad. She heard herself far away. So come, the little girl said. Dream Gracie was crying, but Rosie was still laughing. It's okay, Mama. I'm okay. Dream Gracie reached out, wanting to touch Rosie. Hold onto her. Rosie took her hand. Gracie wished she could stay there forever.

18.

"JUST A FEW MORE WEEKS," NICK SAID, PUTTING HIS HAND ON her cheek. "We'll see each other in a few more weeks."

They stood near the door, Nick's bag sitting on the end of the couch. He was smiling, but Gracie was not. "I wish you could stay here," she whispered.

"I don't know anyone here in Pomroy."

She contemplated this. If she asked herself why she was still here, what could she say? Her work, of course. And Stella. Were they reason enough to be here? She guessed now they had to be. "I know," she said, quietly.

"You could come back, you know."

Gracie didn't say anything. It had been on her mind since she'd returned. All those years spent wishing for more, wanting to get out and live her life someplace new —what would it say about her if she went back now?

"Well," Nick said, lifting his bag from the couch, setting it beside him on the floor. "You know we'd all be thrilled to have you back."

"Maybe not all of you," she said, thinking of her final moments with Finn.

Nick's lopsided grin returned. "You know I can't go if I think you'll be wallowing in self-pity as soon as I leave."

"Well, if that's the case, I'll be wallowing for at least another week."

"Nice try, kid." He replied, wrapping his arms around her. "You're much too strong for that."

She let out a laugh, the kind that comes out when you don't know quite what else to do. They looked at each other, seconds passing by, neither wanting to say goodbye. Finally, Gracie reached up, unhooking the clasp that held her locket in place. "Would you do something for me, Nick?" she asked. She held the locket out to him. He took it, opening it and realizing what she was giving him. "Take it to him for me."

"This is Rosie?" he asked. And for a moment, she was sure she saw tears in his eyes.

Gracie nodded. She knew every curve of her face by now.

"Are you sure you want to give it away?"

"I'm sure."

She could tell he was uncertain. He shifted his weight, still looking at Rosie. "Why?" he asked. "If you don't mind my asking."

"I don't mind." she replied. It was, after all, her most precious possession. The one item that went with her everywhere. She could see why he would question it. "Finn never saw her. Even when I told him about Rosie. He got so angry, I didn't have a chance to show it to him. Maybe seeing her face will help him heal from all this, give him closure. At the very least, maybe it will help him feel close to her."

"She's an angel, Gracie," he said.

She smiled, knowing he was right.

"So, you'll take it to him?"

"Of course." He closed the locket and strung it around his neck. "I'll wear it home so I don't lose it," he said, tucking it into his shirt. The clock he had bought for her was ticking methodically along, the only sound in the apartment until he reached down and picked up his bag once again.

"I'm glad you came," Gracie said, opening the door for him.

"Me too."

They hugged once more. Nick turned to go, but Gracie grabbed for his arm. "Nick, you've got to tell H. When you get back, go tell her. She deserves to know who you are."

He nodded. Gracie pictured Hannah, finding out she had a brother. She suddenly wished she could be there to see it.

"You take care, Gracie."

"I will, Nick."

"You'll be okay now?" he asked.

"I'll be alright. You just make sure that locket gets to Finn."

He turned, then, walking to the stairs and disappearing down them, out of sight. She stood in the doorway, unmoving. Her skin was sticky from the humidity and she reached up, lifting her hair off her shoulders and securing it into a ponytail. She turned back into her apartment, shutting the door behind her, thankful for the air conditioner that had been running nonstop since her return to Pomroy. With her hair off her neck, and her necklace gone, she felt bare, and she reached up, feeling the spot where the locket used to rest. She imagined Finn opening it for the first time, wishing she had been the one to show it to him. Wishing she hadn't been so foolish to have run off in the first place. Even so, Nick was right. She couldn't hate herself forever. She had to forgive herself for the things she'd done.

She walked into the kitchen, getting a glass down and filling it with ice before turning on the faucet and letting the water fill to the top. She took a big gulp, the ice hitting her top lip as she tilted the glass.

She heard a knock at the door. "Gracie?"

"Stella?" She set down the cup and walked back to the door, opening it wide. "What are you doing here?"

"I have some news. Are you busy? Is your brother still here?" She looked around the apartment, inspecting it.

"No, he just left. I'm surprised you didn't see him in the parking lot."

"Oh, no, I didn't see anyone."

"Can I get you a glass of water?" she asked, walking back to the kitchen.

"Actually, that sounds great. It's a scorcher out there."

"It really is," Gracie said, filling up another glass and handing it to her friend.

Stella walked over to the couch, sitting down and kicking up her feet onto the coffee table. She was dressed in pink scrubs, and Gracie guessed she had just finished a shift. "So, what's your news?"

The older woman took a deep breath, setting her glass down and clasping her hands together. Her eyes sparkled, and she looked happy in the way that newlyweds look when they've finally said their "I Dos" and been pronounced man and wife. "I'm moving."

Gracie was stunned. As far as she knew, Stella had always lived in Pomroy. "Moving?"

Stella's face fell. "Aw, honey," she said, realizing Gracie's dismay. "This is a good thing."

"I'm sorry," Gracie said, forcing a smile. "Tell me everything." She sat down next to Stella, who was barely able to contain her excitement.

"They offered me early retirement."

"Offered it?"

"Well, you know how it goes..." she said, waving off Gracie's inquisition. "It doesn't matter. I've found a little place, out in South Carolina, right along the beach. It's small, but it's just me. I can buy it right out, live by the water. It's the American dream, right?"

"I suppose it is."

"My own little piece of paradise."

The sound of the clock filled the room again. "You won't know anyone," Gracie said, her eyes on Stella.

"I'll make friends," Stella said, matter-of-factly. "And..."

"What?" Gracie asked, wondering what could possibly have made Stella think this was a good idea.

"You could come with me."

"You're kidding, right?"

"We could be roommates. There's a hospital not far from town that needs nurses. I'm thinking of volunteering there. You could apply, and even if you didn't get something right away, the house is paid for. Can you imagine anything better than living off of the beach? I've dreamed of it my whole life." Gracie swallowed, not sure what to say. It may have been Stella's dream, but was it hers?

"Stella, are you serious?"

"I am."

"I can't go to South Carolina," she said, finally.

Stella smiled. "I thought you might say that." She hesitated, mulling over whether to say her next words. "Can you tell me why?"

Gracie pictured herself walking along the beach, her toes in the sand. She could almost hear the waves hitting the shore. *Almost.* "I think I need to go home."

Stella stood, holding out her arms, and Gracie moved from the couch, falling into them. "Well, this is perfect timing, then," Stella said into her ear. She pulled away and looked into Stella's eyes, realizing that she had known this was coming and had probably known for a very long time.

"When are you leaving?" Gracie asked.

"One week."

"So soon?"

"You can't keep the beach waiting, can you?"

She laughed, hugging her friend again. "No, I reckon you can't."

Stella's face grew serious. "When are you going to put in your notice?"

"Tomorrow, after my shift ends."

"That soon?" Stella asked.

Gracie thought of Hannah. She thought of Nick, driving back to Ashland with her locket. She thought of Cayla, about to celebrate another birthday, with more days in between that she was missing. She thought of Finn.

"You can't keep your life waiting, Stella."

Gracie picked up the box sitting by the door. She reached over, flipping off the light and opened the door. She didn't look back, didn't cry any tears leaving it behind. As she walked to the car after locking it up, she felt nothing but relief.

It had never been home. No matter how much she had hoped to make it that.

Home was seven hours away. Home was her family. That she had tried so desperately to deny those feelings, baffled her now. She knew it was where she was supposed to be with every part of her.

She climbed into her car and turned on the AC. The vents were already pointing in her direction and she let the cool air blast her, relishing the coldness on her face.

Slowly, she drove the car out of the parking lot, out of Pomroy.

She thought of Stella, who was now relaxing with a view of a beautiful beach shoreline. She cared for Stella deeply, and while she would miss her friend, she knew it was not goodbye. They would see each other again.

The landscape faded away as she drove, listening to the voices on the radio sing about lost loves, tortured relationships and all the things that make the heart beat and emotions run wild.

In a few hours, she would be back where she started, figuring out her next move. She had a job interview at the hospital in Ashland next week. Hannah and Dave were letting her stay a few more weeks while she looked for her own place. She'd been so excited at Gracie's revelation that she'd screamed and dropped her phone when Gracie told her she was coming back for good. And just like that she knew it was the right decision.

Finn still hadn't answered any of her calls. Nick had given him the necklace over a week ago, calling to let her know that he hadn't responded when he slid it in an envelope that read *From Gracie* under the door.

Her hand went again to the spot where her locket used to hang, and she thought of Rosie. No matter what happened, there was comfort in knowing she and Finn had created such perfection. That somehow, someday they might see her again. Finn might not forgive her in this life, but they'd made Rosie, together, and that was something special. No one could take that from her.

The further she got from Pomroy's city limits, the lighter she felt. On the seat beside her was her purse, and through the top, you could just see the old switchblade sticking out. She remembered Finn, making her climb up the ladder in the barn first, already looking out for her, and she said a silent prayer that somewhere inside he still felt compelled to do so.

The road kept winding, and she pushed on the accelerator. She'd never dwelled on the bad events in her life. She'd always pushed through, forging on, a soldier with no side to fight on. But she had a side now. She knew exactly what she wanted, and she was ready to fight for it if it came to that.

Yes, if it came to that, she would be ready.

Her future was worth the fight. Finn was worth the fight.

She was worth the fight.

The apartment was small, but clean. Gracie looked over her shoulder at Olivia, who shrugged, then stepped around the leasing agent. She turned, looking out the window in the direction of Finn's apartment, wondering what he was doing, where he was at this exact moment.

"I'll give you two a minute to look around. I've got to return a phone call quickly and then I'll be back to give you all the details on this place."

"Thanks," Gracie mumbled, running her hand on the kitchen counter.

"What do you think?" Olivia asked, leaning against the wall.

The apartment was fine, but she still felt unsure about it. Signing a lease felt too much like giving up on Finn.

"How is he?" Gracie asked, unable to meet Olivia's eyes when she asked the question.

"Finn?"

Gracie nodded.

"I really don't know," she answered, truthfully. "We haven't seen him since you left. He won't even return Grant's phone calls."

This surprised her. Finn wasn't even talking to his closest friends?

Olivia straightened out and took a deep breath. "Did something happen at the market after we left?" Gracie could tell she was treading carefully, not wanting to overstep whatever boundary she might be crossing by asking, but unable to keep quiet about it any longer.

She felt her head grow heavy and placed it in her hands. When she looked up, Olivia immediately took one of her hands.

"I told him why I left."

"And he was..." she hesitated, trying to read Gracie's face. "Angry?"

"Very much so." Why did it get harder to tell people about Rosie? Wasn't being honest supposed to get easier? "Liv, I was pregnant when I left. He didn't know." Olivia, who was still holding her hand, squeezed it tightly. "We had a daughter, Rosie, but she died. She was stillborn."

Olivia's hand pulled away, and she immediately enveloped Gracie, holding her tight. "Damn you, Gracie Mae Brannen," she said. And then, Gracie could tell she was crying. She couldn't move, but she felt her own tears well up.

"I'm sorry I didn't tell you..."

"No. Do not apologize to me." Olivia let go of her and took a step back, looking into Gracie's eyes. "What happened to you...no matter what choices you made...

God, I can't even imagine it. I can't..." She stopped, and Gracie realized it was the first time that she had seen Olivia this upset.

"Liv, he said he wanted us to be together. He told me at the market. It was my last chance to be honest with him before I left and headed back to Pomroy. If you'd seen the look on his face, what he must have thought of me..."

"Shhh," Olivia whispered. She took hold of Gracie's shoulders, her fingers squeezing the skin tightly. "I'm sure it's just the shock of it."

"That's what Hannah said, but I don't know..."

"Well, I do. Finn Miller has been in love with you his whole life."

Gracie wiped a tear away, studying her friend. "I was so selfish."

"You were scared. And then..." She paused. "And then you were heartbroken."

"It wasn't right."

Olivia shook her head. "Neither is having to say goodbye to your baby before you've even said hello."

The door slammed, causing them to snap their heads towards it as the leasing agent stepped back into the apartment. "Any questions?" she asked.

"No, I think we're done looking for today, but thanks so much for your help." Olivia's voice was rushed and she grabbed for Gracie's hand, leading her around the agent and back into the hallway. Once they were outside, she turned to Gracie, her hands on her hips. "I can't let you rent this place. You've got to reach out to Finn again before you move into some crappy apartment by yourself. And anyway, doesn't Hannah want you living with her?"

"Of course she says she doesn't mind, but she's busy with Cayla and I'm in Cayla's room. Their house isn't that big, Liv."

"Well, what about Finn?"

"I've tried. I've called. I've texted. I've done everything I can do. His last words to me were 'I never want to see you again.' I think I need to take the hint."

"Take the hint? Really? If that's what you think you are doing, why did you even move back?"

Gracie shrugged.

"You came back here to fight, Gracie. To fight for Finn. You're showing him you want to be with him."

"He doesn't even know I'm back for good, yet, Olivia."

"You didn't tell him?"

"I thought I would when he picked up, but he never did."

Olivia whipped out her phone and started tapping on the screen. "Well, we can solve that problem right now."

19.

THREE DAYS LATER, GRACIE STILL HADN'T HEARD FROM FINN, but Olivia had received a text from him a few hours later. It had read, *Stay out of it, Liv.* Olivia had called her to let her know, fuming about a man's pride, but Gracie knew it was more than that. It was betrayal and heartbreak. In the same breath that Rosie had been a possibility, she had also been taken away.

Gracie turned up the gravel road into the cemetery, her feet moving swiftly beneath her, reading the names of the headstones as she walked. It was gloomy, with a chance for storms later on in the day. Fitting for a trip to the cemetery, she thought. Her mother's plot had yet to get its own headstone. Instead there were a few cut flowers and a stake with her name on it in bold black lettering. She thought of Mama's handwriting, the swirly way she jotted down lists. She was always making lists—one for Hannah's chores, one for Gracie's, the grocery list, the work shifts list, the birthday list. The birthday list was always Mama's favorite. It grew every year as Mama found out new birthdays. A neighbor here. A co-worker there. She kept track of them all and at the very least made a birthday phone call.

She knelt down, letting her gaze fall over the words— Here lies Sarah Elizabeth Brannen.

"Oh Mama," she whispered.

She closed her eyes, picturing the last day they were together, when she'd been walking back from Finn's.

She'd been so distraught at the time, consumed by her own thoughts, she hadn't *really* seen her mother that day, and she found herself wishing she had looked at her— really looked at her. A bird flew overhead and Gracie looked up, watching it soar in circles high above her head before swooping down and disappearing into the wooded brush surrounding the cemetery. Mama had always been in the background of her life. She'd been busy working and busy trying to protect the girls from their father. Gracie knew it hadn't been easy for her. Still, she wished they had been closer, the way Mama and Hannah were.

She thought of the day she left. The house had been quiet—both Mama and Hannah at work. She'd already packed a bag and decided on her destination. She remembered the apprehension, the sadness, looking around the house. While one part of her wanted to stay, the other was already in Pomroy, figuring out her next move. She'd placed a hand on her stomach and looked down, rubbing it back and forth, and she knew she'd never let anyone make Rosie feel the way she felt when her daddy looked at her. While she knew that Finn was completely unlike him, she knew babies changed people. She knew Mama hadn't fallen in love with a heartless cheat. No, that man she fell in love with had been changed by life, by their circumstances. When she thought of it, she knew it would kill her to watch that happen to Finn.

So, she'd packed up the car, leaving a note on the kitchen counter, and drove out of Glenwood. The crunch of gravel beneath the tires rang in her ears as she pulled out, driving out of the one place she'd ever called home.

"I'm so sorry," she whispered. "I wish I had come back sooner. I wish I had known you were sick." She reached out and touched the nameplate, tracing the writing with her fingers. "You were a good mama to us. I never told you that, and I know you thought you didn't do enough, but you did what you could." She paused, tears springing to her eyes as she choked out her next words. "Please take care of our Rosie, and tell her that I miss her. That I love her. That she's always in my thoughts. Can you do that for me?"

But of course there was no answer and all Gracie could do then was put her head in her hands and cry for the time she would never get back, for the mistakes she made and for the unknown future that awaited her.

"Gracie," Finn said, nudging her playfully. "You're a bit out of it today." He sat up on the bed and took her hand.

"Just thinkin'," she said, not looking at him. She hadn't been able to look him in the eye all day.

He sighed, then jumped to his feet. "Just a few more days and we're out of here."

"Yeah," Gracie said, her voice shaky.

"I know it's a bit scary," he said, noticing her less than enthusiastic response. "But this is what we've always wanted."

We have, haven't we, she thought.

She hesitated, knowing her next words wouldn't be what he wanted to hear. "Finn, what if we stayed?" She was right. His face fell.

"You've never wanted to stay in Glenwood. You hate it here."

"That's not true."

"Yes it is."

"Well, what if I changed my mind?"

Finn crossed his arms in front of him. "What's going on, Gracie?

"What do you mean?"

"I mean you're changing your mind at the very last minute now? This is something we've talked about since we were kids."

"I know, but maybe college isn't for me. You know, I'm not a great student..."

"You're great at the stuff you're interested in." His voice became softer, more reassuring. "You're just getting nervous, but you don't need to be. We have each other."

Any thoughts of college were far from her mind now. All she could think about was the two pink lines she'd seen just this morning.

She felt sick. Finn was right about one thing, though. She was scared.

"Finn, how do you know you want to be with me?"

"What?" He held up his hands in disbelief. "How can you even ask that?"

"Don't you ever wonder if you're just with me by default?"

He looked annoyed. "What does that even mean? By default."

"You know. It's a small town. Not many other options."

"That's the most ridiculous thing I've ever heard," he said, his eyes narrowing at her. They were quiet a moment longer before he sighed, then kissed her. "I love you."

Gracie looked away, feeling guilty. "But there are so many experiences you haven't had. How do you know?"

"I just do."

Finn wasn't going to make this easy. "Okay, so can't we be together here? In Glenwood?"

He shook his head. "No, Gracie. We can't get sucked in here. We've always talked about leaving and we're going to do it."

Maybe it could work, she thought. The two of them could still leave and she could just get a job somewhere until the baby came. It could work. She tried to picture it, the two of them getting by somehow. It seemed impossible.

Finn got up and walked across the room. "If we stay here, you'll end up pregnant and I'll end up working some low-wage job for the rest of my life. Is that what you want?" He turned to look at her.

"No," she whispered.

"Everything will be fine," he said. "We just have to stick to the plan."

Gracie tried to smile, but it took more effort than it should have.

"Finn, I need to tell you something."

She braced herself, preparing for his reaction.

"Do *you* want to see other people?" he asked.

Startled, she looked up at him. "No," she whispered. "I love you."

"Then start getting excited. That's all I want."

"What if I can't do that?"

To Gracie's surprise, Finn smiled. "You've never been good at letting go." He ran his fingers through her hair. "You've got to believe there's more out there for us. I do."

"I want to believe that," she said, not knowing what to say or how to feel. She stood up, dazed. "I better get home." She turned to the door, her mind racing. She needed to tell him and she needed to do it now. If she left, she would lose all her courage. "Finn..." She turned back to look at him.

"Gracie." He interrupted her, standing up to meet her gaze. "Go home. Pack your stuff. Let these doubts go. We're going to do better than this. We're getting out of here, you hear?"

She nodded. He kissed her head. She left the room, walking slowly. *Go back!* Her mind screamed as her legs moved forward. *Go back and tell him!*

But she kept walking. She walked all the way home until she saw Mama there, waiting for her. What was she doing here? Did she know? Mama didn't say a word, just reached her arm around Gracie's shoulders and pulled her tight. Gracie slumped against her, putting more weight on Mama than she should have, but Mama held her up.

They approached the house, and she looked up. She could see her future life here. If she stayed, she'd just be repeating Mama's life. She'd be trapped. For the first time that day, she felt like she was thinking clearly. She'd leave Glenwood, but by herself. She walked inside, leaving Mama on the porch. She reached down, putting a hand on her belly as she walked into her bedroom, closing the door behind her. Quickly, she pulled out her suitcase and started packing up her stuff. She stopped once, hesitating, thinking of Finn. They loved each other. Could she really just leave with his child growing inside her? She looked up, towards the door, remembering the screaming from the living room as Daddy drank bottle after bottle. Remembering the fear and hate she had felt for so many days and nights as it grew worse and worse. That was not going to be her life. Finn didn't want a baby now. He'd said as much himself. There was only one thing to do.

She turned back to her suitcase, putting the last of her clothes into it, then opened the top drawer of her dresser. Hidden underneath a stack of tank tops, it sat. The switchblade. She tossed it into the suitcase then sat down on the bed. No, she couldn't take it with her. If she did, it would be like she was leaving for good. She'd come back. Once the baby was here, she'd come back. She picked the switchblade up, then walked to the closet and pulled down a box tucked up on the top shelf. She opened it, then set the blade on top. She closed her eyes, squeezing them so tight no tears could escape. It wasn't goodbye. Not forever, she told herself. She'd be back. Someday.

20.

GRACIE'S EARLIEST MEMORY WITH FINN WAS AT FOUR YEARS old. They were riding their bikes around their neighborhood and one of Gracie's training wheels got stuck in the mud. Finn started laughing, and hopped down off of his bike to help her, but she was so mad he was laughing at her that she kicked him down as he came close, forcing him back into the muddy puddle surrounding them. He'd gotten back on his own bike and pedaled home, leaving her there to figure out how to get her bike free. She'd walked home alone, wondering if she'd lost her best friend forever. She'd cried to Hannah before bed that night, feeling terrible for kicking him. But, Finn hadn't stayed mad for long. He'd come by the house the very next day, asking if she wanted to play in the treehouse. Once they'd climbed up, he apologized for laughing at her and, in his words, "deserving to get pummeled into the ground." She shouldn't have doubted herself. Finn always came around, in the end. But would he today?

"You okay?" Hannah asked as she approached the kitchen. Her older sister was putting the finishing touches on Cayla's birthday cake.

"I am," she replied, picking up the box of birthday candles. She tapped them up and down on the counter.

"Would you hand me that yellow icing there?" Hannah asked. She looked up from the cake as Gracie handed it to her. "You're fidgety. You shouldn't be. He'll come."

"He hates me."

Hannah stopped what she was doing. "You know he doesn't."

"All I know is what I did. And the way he looked at me. All I know is the pain I've caused everyone. I wouldn't blame him."

"He would blame himself. I think he has this whole time you've been gone. And if he wanted to move on from you, he would have. He could have, you know."

Gracie nodded. "I hope you're right."

Hannah slid the last of the yellow frosting onto a spoon and handed it to her sister. "Here," she said. "A little sugar never hurt anyone."

Gracie tasted it, feeling the sugar crystals on her tongue. "You made this?" she asked.

"From scratch. No store-bought frosting for my kid. Are you kidding? We Brannen girls do things right when it comes to sweets."

"It's amazing," she said, watching as Hannah put a few toothpicks in the cake and covered it with saran wrap.

The doorbell rang and Hannah hurried from the kitchen. Gracie followed her out, still licking the spoon.

When she opened the door, Nick was standing there holding a gift wrapped in wrapping paper decorated with an array of kittens in party hats.

"Happy Birthday, my darling girl," he said as Cayla ran up to him and jumped in his arms.

"Uncle Nick, do you know how old I am?"

Nick pretended to think about it then said, "I don't know. Forty-five?"

Cayla giggled, tilting her head back. "No!" She grabbed his face and playfully shook his head in her hands. "I'm seven!"

"Seven?!" he laughed. "You're almost the same age as me."

"Uncle Nick, I don't think so," she responded, still smiling.

Nick put Cayla down and gave Hannah a hug. "Saving any for us?" he asked, spotting Gracie finishing off the icing on her spoon.

"I'm not big on sharing my sweets," she said as Nick leaned in to embrace her.

"There's plenty of sugar to come," Hannah said before disappearing into the kitchen again. "People will be here soon. Would you guys set up some tables and chairs out in the backyard?"

"We will get right to it," Gracie said.

"How's the apartment hunting going?" Nick asked.

"It's going...nowhere."

"Well, maybe I'll have to help you with that. Or, maybe you have someone helping?" His expression turned hopeful.

"If you mean Finn, then no. I still haven't heard from him."

"Is he coming today?"

Gracie shook her head as Hannah called from the kitchen, "He's coming."

"Hannah has more faith than I do," Gracie said.

"Who's coming, Uncle Nick?" Cayla asked, emerging between them.

"Oh, everyone. Aren't they? Who would miss the birthday party of this little princess?"

"I see who the favorite is now," Gracie said, winking at Nick.

"I have lots of favorites," Cayla said, putting her arms up around each of their waists.

"As you should," Nick said. "Well, you heard your mom. Let's get those tables set up."

Olivia and Grant showed up next, right as they finished securing the balloon banner to the entryway. Friends of Cayla from school appeared next, followed by other friends of Hannah and Dave. Each time the door swung open, Gracie's head snapped toward it to see who had entered, and each time she turned to Nick who gave her a sympathetic look. Hannah continuously walked by and gave her a gentle pat on the shoulder, whispering "He'll be here" in her ear.

When Cayla ripped into her first gift, Gracie's eyes went to the front door. When everyone began to sing, Gracie felt herself inch closer to the window, her eyes searching for him through it. And when Hannah cut into the cake, she finally let it sink in that he wasn't coming.

Her chest heaved a bit and she felt a sob begin to rise up. It hit her so quickly, she almost didn't catch it. Embarrassed, she slipped into the hallway to compose herself. This was Cayla's day. But her heart wouldn't reconcile with her head. She couldn't focus, couldn't form a coherent thought to calm herself down. In that moment, tears streaming down her face, she felt the weight of her choice and the sorrow she had carried with her for all these years, deep in her soul.

Laughter reverberated through the house, forcing its way to her ears and fighting against the hollowness that now came to rest inside her. She wiped her face, closed her eyes and took a deep breath. A moment later, Cayla came into the hall, tentatively taking in her aunt's demeanor.

"Aunt Gracie?" she said, her small fingers wrapping around a strand of her hair as she peered up at her distraught aunt. "Are you okay?"

Gracie forced the corners of her mouth to turn in the other direction. She nodded, almost too enthusiastically. "I'm great," she said, shaking her head profusely. She let out a staggered breath. "I'm so happy to be here for your birthday."

Cayla's eyes bored into her and Gracie felt exposed. "Let's get back to your party, okay?"

But Cayla didn't turn around as she moved her body to pass by, causing Gracie to stop mid-step.

"Aunt Gracie, are you going to leave again?" she asked, her eyes beginning to fill with tears.

"What?"

Cayla fidgeted with her party hat, pulling the thin white string from her chin and tracing it back and forth. "Because Finn didn't come?"

Gracie clutched her hands together and knelt down to Cayla's level. "No," she said. "Of course not."

"I wished for him to come," the little girl said. "I wished he would for my birthday wish. I don't want you to go."

"Oh, Cayla," Gracie pulled her into her arms, wondering if her emotions were that obvious or if Cayla just happened to be particularly perceptive today. "I'm not going anywhere."

"But you're sad," she said. "Isn't that why you left before?" Cayla straightened up to look at her.

"You're right. I am sad. But that's not why I left before. Not completely, anyway."

"Why, then?"

Gracie sighed and thought for a minute. "I guess it was mostly because I was scared."

"Of Finn?"

Gracie almost laughed. "No, not of him. For him. And for me." She pulled Cayla to her again, this time to reassure her. "I'm not scared anymore, Cayla."

It seemed to be what Cayla wanted to hear. "Okay."

"Hey, what are you two doing over here? A few people are heading out and want to see you before they go." Hannah stopped when she noticed the looks on their faces. "Everything alright?"

Cayla nodded, taking Gracie's hand in hers. "Yep," she said, then led Gracie past her mom so they could say their goodbyes.

"What's she doing here?"

Gracie heard Finn's voice in the next room. When he hadn't shown up to the party, Olivia had taken one look at her melancholy friend and decided enough was enough. "He's got to talk to you," she'd said, exasperated, and sent Grant to call him after the party had ended and they'd retreated back to Olivia and Grant's. Now, her entire body trembled, but she stood in Olivia and Grant's doorway, strong as the substantial maple tree in the front yard.

A few seconds later, Finn appeared in the kitchen where Olivia and Gracie stood. Grant entered, just a few steps behind him.

"I just want a chance to talk to you," Gracie said. "To explain..."

Finn looked from Gracie to Olivia and back again as if he were trying to decide who to blame for this unexpected meeting. Finally, he sighed and said, "Fine. Outside."

When both she and Finn had made their way out of the house, she closed the door behind her and followed Finn to the far edge of the yard where they'd have some privacy. He walked in long strides and she struggled to keep up with him.

He stopped near the fire pit and turned, his hands on his hips, waiting.

Silence filled the space between them until Gracie coughed to clear her throat. "How are you?" she asked.

In that moment, she saw something in him change.

"What?" she asked, feeling unsure of herself and wanting him to speak.

"I don't know," he said.

"I thought you were going to yell at me."

He stood across from her, somewhat dumbfounded. "I thought I was going to yell at you, too."

"But now you're not?"

"No," he said. "I looked up and I saw you. Not you here. I mean, not you now, today. I saw you then."

She studied him, confused.

"I saw you...that night. The one when we ran from your house...after your..." Finn sighed. "I said I'd kill him if he hurt you."

"I remember." Gracie wasn't sure what he was trying to say.

"I'm hurting you," he said. "Right now."

"Well, I hurt you first if I remember right."

He shook his head, like what she'd said didn't matter at all. "This isn't who I am," he said.

Gracie wrapped her arms around herself. "It's because of me..."

He walked towards her. "It's because of you I ever did anything, felt anything. I don't want to yell at you, Gracie. All I've ever wanted to do was give you what you gave me."

"What did I ever give to you? If anything, I took so much away from you."

It only took Finn a second to answer. "You gave me a different way to see things." And then, because he could tell she didn't believe him, he added, "You know, some things just can't be explained," Finn said. "That's you and me. It just is what it is."

"It's something I didn't understand," she said.

"I don't think I always understood it, either," he said. "That pull to you. I just knew I needed you. Maybe we would have hated each other after what happened with Rosie. Maybe that's *why* you left."

"But I didn't know what would happen to her."

Finn took her hand in his. "No, I'm not saying you knew and so you left. I'm saying, maybe in this crazy, messed-up world, the universe said, the death of their daughter is enough to pull them apart..."

"...and so it somehow got me to run off before it could happen?" Gracie, skeptical, couldn't hide her doubts.

"Maybe it was easier for us than pulling each other out of our grief."

"I don't know. I don't think the universe is so concerned with our feelings."

Finn squeezed her hands, then locked his fingers in hers. "I'm sorry," he said, his head lolling back. "I said all the wrong things. I didn't hear you that night. I should have."

"I didn't tell you..."

"But, Gracie, I've always known what you were feeling. You shouldn't have had to tell me. I knew when you were scared to go home because you never knew what you would find there. I knew when you watched Liv with her cheer friends how you wished you could find a way to relate to them the way she did. You didn't tell me that, but I knew. And I knew you wanted more than anything to get out of Glenwood, too. It was completely out of character for you to suddenly want to stay and I'm kicking myself for ignoring such an obvious sign."

"It's not your fault. I'm the one who hurt you over and over again," she said, feeling almost frantic. Was he forgiving her for everything?

"You did what you thought you had to do," he said, matter-of-factly. He pulled her into him, hugging her close. "Rosie wouldn't want me to hate you for trying to protect her. I can still be a good father to her," he paused to look at her, his eyes filled with pride, and with the hurt of never knowing his daughter. "Even if she's not here."

Gracie sighed, then moved her fingers across her cheek, wiping her tears away. "I love you, Finn Miller."

They stood together, unable to part. Gracie, afraid to let go of him now that she finally had him back, leaned into him, unsteady. She hadn't been sure this moment would ever come. She'd been preparing herself to leave Finn Miller behind her.

Again.

But he'd never really belonged in her past, had he? Once upon a time, Finn had been her future. And she realized, with a childlike wonder, he was still her future.

Even now, after everything. And it reminded her of a song she'd once heard, with the melody of a long-lost dream.

Around them, the leaves rustled, constructing their own song to sing, and Gracie let the sound envelop her. She had come a long way to get here, to find her way back. It had probably taken too long. But none of that mattered now. Breathing in deep, she closed her eyes and believed it: she was finally home.

The End.

Acknowledgements

First, thank you to my readers. Without your support, this novel may have taken much longer to be published. Thank you for helping me to continue doing what I love. To Hanna Piepel, Elizabeth Keest Sedrel, Lauren Denton and Guido Henkel, thank you for your ongoing kindness throughout this process, as well as for contributing your own talents to *Gracie's Song*. To my family and friends, I am grateful for your love and encouraging words...but mostly I'm grateful I got lucky enough to have you in my life. You are all home to me.

About the Author

MICHELLE SCHLICHER is the author of the novel
The Blue Jay. A graduate of Iowa State University, she
subsequently worked for six years in communications and
marketing. She lives in a suburb of Des Moines with her
husband and two children.
Interested in learning about future releases? You can find
me at:

michelleschlicher.com

instagram.com/michelleschlicher

facebook.com/michelleschlicherbooks

twitter.com/chelleschlicher

If you enjoyed this book, please consider leaving an
honest review on Amazon and/or Goodreads.